WHITE NOISE

THE MALLET

P A WILSON

Ebook ISBN: 978-1-990509-10-0
Paperback ISBN: 978-1-990509-11-7
Audio book ISBN:978-1-990509-12-4

FREE EBOOK

Claim your copy of Running the Game when you use the QR code below to sign up for my newsletter and cheer on Pen as she vies for a commission in the military.

1

---

ofie sat across from Dr. Bindes at his usual table at the back of the Open Pit. She resisted the urge to turn and look for anyone leaning too close, or even staring at them. Being here was a risk in itself because she had no reason to visit him outside a legit clinic. She had to trust he was as worried about observation as she was.

"What changed your mind?" he asked. "You were adamant that the operation was a no-go."

Fear. She didn't want to admit it aloud, but the few days she'd had off after the last case had been filled with dread, waiting for the next attack of the Fades. The meds were not working well enough, and if she was experiencing symptoms when she was relaxing, it was only a matter of time before she had a full-on attack in front of her boss.

"You should be happy I agreed," she said. "You've been nagging me about it since I met you. Have you changed your mind? Has some miracle drug been invented so I don't need the operation?"

It all came out so cranky she almost apologized. But that

would make her sound weak and that was the last thing she needed him thinking.

"Nope, the operation is the only way to cure the Fades. When will you have time?"

Never. "I'll just book when you have an opening. No major case on my plate right now. I just need a bit of notice."

He looked her over. "Let's go in the back so I can assess you." He stood and headed for the small room he used as a clinic for his patients.

Sofie didn't move. Too many visits to the back room might be noticed.

He stood at the door. "Sofie, come on. I promise it won't hurt. You'll be out of here in ten minutes."

She slid out of the booth and looked around as she turned to join him. No one was paying any attention. Maybe they'd just gotten used to Bindes receiving odd visitors. Maybe some of them were waiting for their turn with the only decent doctor offering unregistered medical help. The Fades wasn't the only condition on the Mallet that could make it difficult to keep a job once reported.

In the office, Bindes checked her breathing and blood pressure. He didn't comment on either. Then he took a blood sample and placed it in a scanner. "That will take a bit. So, assuming everything is okay, how about in four or five days?"

She laughed. "Before I change my mind?"

"Before you get too busy and have a good excuse to cancel," he said. "Well?"

"How long do I have to be off?" Now that she'd made the decision, she wanted it over.

"Before you come in, you need to fast for twelve hours. I'm counting on you doing that at work. We'll plan the procedure for the evening shift."

"Total fasting? Like nothing but water?"

"Stim-juice is fine, just no heavy flavoring."

"I can do that. I'm more worried about taking time off."

"How are the meds working?" Bindes asked as he checked something on his pad.

"They aren't. I'm taking twice as many as I should."

The machine beeped. Bindes checked the results and nodded to himself. "Okay, don't get sick in the next five days. Come here at end of shift and I'll take you to the clinic. You should be recovered in three days."

"And if I can't get that many days off? I'm not planning to go back to work until I'm ready, but shit happens. If I get called back in, what do I do?" Having to explain she was recovering from surgery that wouldn't show up on her records would be as bad as declaring she had the Fades in the first place. "I mean, you can put something in my records to explain the surgery, right?"

"You want me to arrange that?"

She almost said yes, but then thought through the ramifications. "No. Too many ways for that to go wrong. And too many people involved in covering it up. I don't like owing anyone a favor."

"You need a day. Just one, but you'll be in pain, and you can't take anything for it. You'll have to avoid excessive physical activity because if you dislodge the device, you could lose your sight or ability to speak."

And then it wouldn't be long before she was dumped in for processing into nutrients or spaced like any other dead body. Volunteering to do desk work wouldn't fly if they called her in on a case. She would have to deal with the situation if it came up. Sofie didn't hold out any hope that things on the Mallet would stay calm for more than five minutes.

"Okay. Whatever I have on my plate now will be cleared in the next five days. Anything else?"

"The meds," Bindes said. "It's not just yours. I'm seeing more of my patients deteriorating, at the legit clinic and here. The expiry dates must be wrong. I don't know why it's happening. We're prescribing stuff that should be good for a year or more, and they are running at half strength or less."

"Why would someone fix dates?"

"The usual. Money or power. But it could be other reasons. People do dangerous things for the worst and best reasons. Someone looking for vengeance, or just wanting to kill one person and hide the murder with a lot of collateral damage. Because they think they are saving us from some horrible fate by winnowing the gene pool."

Not great for anyone. "Can you find out anything else without getting caught?"

Bindes put his pad to the side and looked at her for a moment. Then with a shrug, he said, "I'll try, but you're the cop."

And a victim. "It would be easier if someone reported it." She shook her head when he started to protest. "I said it would be easier. But I get that you can't. I'll do what I can, but official cases will take precedence, and I don't have a lot of spare time now that I'm prepping for an operation."

"I could reschedule your surgery. Sofie, not everyone can choose a permanent fix for their condition. Sometimes the meds are the only way to manage."

I don't need a guilt trip right now. "I said I'd do what I can. What about the Elites? Any chance they might be affected?"

"That's more like it. Yes, the Mallet doesn't discriminate with chronic conditions. And maybe it's an Elite doing it."

2

Elites would do almost anything to gain power. Money was the fastest way to increase your control of any and all aspects of life on the Mallet. Sofie believed that pursuit was tempered by the fact that the lower castes in Maintenance and Manufacturing were assets. Not important enough to be treated to a comfortable life. But replacing people cost money, probably more money than a couple of generations of workers could earn. If an Elite family was messing with the medications that kept people working, then something fundamental had changed without her noticing.

Sofie's attention snapped back to her surroundings as a low rumble of voices intruded on her thoughts. The trip between work and the Open Pit usually didn't require her to be fully aware of the world around her because most people were hurrying to or from work shifts. Today, people gathered in groups talking, mostly quietly, but the occasional shout made the conversations pause. She scanned the area. Some of the small shops and cafes were shuttered. The groups were moving together. The orange badges with the word *enough* in blue made a big statement in large numbers. She was the only cop in sight and if violence sparked, she wouldn't be able to stop even the smallest confrontation.

Two larger groups formed as the crowds came together. They weren't facing her, but Sofie caught a few glances from the periphery. She couldn't stop what was happening, but she could listen. And report. She placed her hand in her pocket and tapped a code on her pad without looking. In seconds, Captain Llewelyn would know to be on alert, and everything that happened until she entered a second code would be transmitted to his screen. Leaving her pad in her pocket meant only audio, but it left both hands free, and no one would know they were providing evidence against themselves and their friends.

She moved closer to the crowd to catch the conversation. The participants weren't cohesive. On the edges they were arguing the need to protest. So not a planned riot, but the right fuel for one to ignite.

"We should wait until there's proof," a woman said to her companion.

"When people die, it'll be too late," her companion, a young man, said. "People are sick. They aren't on the line. We have to work longer hours. We'll get injured."

"But people get sick all the time," the woman said when he ran out of breath. "How do you know this is different?"

The man looked at her in surprise. "You don't believe? Look, if you still have questions, just go. We only need people who are committed. If you've bought the Elites' lies, I can't help you."

Sofie moved away before capturing the woman's answer or being noticed.

"My sister is in the clinic," a man said. "She was fine one day, and then too sick to work."

"Where are the headlines?" another man growled. "No one cares if we die until the production numbers drop."

But a big protest should draw the media. Sofie scanned the edges of the crowd for cameras. None close enough to get pulled down if things went wrong, but a few drones in the air to get background shots. She noticed two drones that belonged to the police.

She had two choices to get back to the station: work her way through the crowd hoping no one would turn on her, or slip through the dark streets and hope the protests were confined to this square. Both were risky, but she wasn't in any kind of official gear, so if she kept her mouth shut and moved gently between people, the crowd was the best of the two bad options. Some days it seemed like there were no good options on the Mallet.

The mob wasn't moving in any direction. People were drifting between groups, and the comments were about the same in each one she passed. Sofie scanned the groups before moving between them, on alert for a change in the mood and for anyone who looked like a ringleader. There was no center where someone stoked the crowd's emotions, no drift toward a nexus of higher tension. No placards, no chants, nothing that might escalate the situation.

She hoped Llewelyn didn't overreact. That there were no riot-gear-clad officers headed her way. If this was a peaceful griping session — although it felt too organized for that — the cops could easily ignite more passion. That would bring on a sedative mist and she'd fall to the ground with the rest. People got crushed in that kind of situation.

The edge of the crowd came into sight as Sofie dodged around a final cluster of people. The remaining protesters were not yet clumping together for mutual complaining. No wall of riot troops ahead of her. The sight of one or two people leaving the protest gave her hope.

As she stepped past the last straggler, Sofie's shoulders relaxed. It felt like she was finally taking a breath of air and could start to process the comments she'd heard. What if it was about the meds? What if the problem with hers was only the first sign of a bigger conspiracy? It was hard to dismiss the claims about people falling ill. Too easy to check.

She tapped the code to turn off her pad and hurried away from the protest.

3

When she entered the office, Sofie noticed Amanda's desk was empty. Not just no Amanda, but no papers, no personal items, and the screen was off. Rick was at his desk and when she approached, she saw he was reading bulletins.

"What's going on?" she asked. "Amanda transferred out?"

"Nope. You still have to work with her," Rick said. He nodded toward Llewelyn's office. "She's filling in as the captain's aide. Will be for a few months."

Amanda Mwendwa would love that. She played politics well. Sofie grudgingly acknowledged that Amanda was also a good investigator. Her sniping just made her a hard partner to like. "There's some trouble out in Maintenance," Sofie said.

"Yeah, protests." Rick picked his pad up again. "We got your feed. How bad was it really?"

She told him about the comments and how it felt like people were on the verge of more than just chanting.

"Have you heard anything about this sickness?" she

asked. Amanda stepped out of Llewelyn's office and headed toward them.

"We wouldn't get called in unless there was something suspicious," Rick said.

"Sofie," Amanda said, "good work out there. We decided to let them burn out. No point sending in a force and triggering something bigger."

Sofie noticed the *we*. Now Amanda could pretend she was a decision maker. "It seemed to be all about some sickness. Shouldn't we have heard something? A disease on the Mallet is trouble."

"Yeah, there have been some reports. Llewelyn told me we've had a lot of callouts for people malingering that turned out to be legitimate illness. We haven't been asked to investigate yet."

It wasn't a crime to be ill. Malingering would mean a fine. People were fined for all kinds of petty things. It was a way to keep workers owing money so no one got to leave the Mallet. But being ill or injured was just considered a hazard of any job in Maintenance and Manufacturing. Keeping the Mallet running and processing the ore that came in were dangerous jobs.

"You think it will get that far?" Rick asked. "I mean, what would we investigate? The doctors will get people well or call for a quarantine. We could enforce that, but unless someone is making this happen, we have no crime."

"We'll see," Amanda said. "In the meantime, Llewelyn wants us ready to act if the protests get out of hand. I checked and both of you need to upgrade your equipment. Rick, you need to refresh your riot gear training."

"Good timing," Sofie said. "No new cases on our plate at the moment." She'd planned to do a bit of snooping into the medical supply chain. Look for opportunities to manipulate the expiry dates. It would take less than an hour to get new gear fitted and tested, so she'd have some alone time while Rick sat through his riot training refresher.

"I also looked at your paperwork," Amanda said. "You need to complete last week's case-closing documentation. If you've got nothing else to do, I'll see if any of the other teams could use help." She headed for the next cluster of detectives without waiting for comments.

"I liked the last aide better," Sofie said.

"You don't even know his name," Rick said.

"Exactly. He kept to his job and let us do ours. Amanda is going to be filling our days with busywork."

Rick chuckled. "I'll go refresh my training. Must make Amanda happy with me so she won't assign me to patrol."

Sofie checked her schedule and made an appointment with the armory for later. Right now, she had some snooping through databases to do.

4

S ofie pulled up the records on the recent callouts. Doing what was basically a sick leave check on workers was something every cop had to take on, regardless of rank. The only benefit of being a detective and not a uniformed officer was that your schedule rarely cleared up enough to give you time. Regardless of how often the callouts landed on your desk, no one enjoyed it. Sofie, like all the cops she knew, wanted serious cases. Not that she wanted people to be murdered, or badly beaten up, but finding those perpetrators was exciting, and knocking on the doors of people who'd called in sick one too many times wasn't.

The number of records was surprising, and she noticed that there was a steady increase as time passed. A month ago, three calls a day — pretty normal. In the next two weeks, ten, and these last two weeks, thirty. Definitely pointing to something other than malingering.

She listed the names of the people and the officers who had checked on them. Getting the medical history of the targets was easy because of the charge for malingering.

Normally there was a long and complex process to access anything medical. Malingerers lost those rights the moment someone made the accusation.

It took her fifteen minutes to send the file requests. The system responded with a one-hour estimate for results. Something was taxing the query queue. Probably getting the identities of the protesters.

She turned off her screen so no one would see her searches. Too early to head to the armory for her gear upgrade, and with the mess outside, not a good idea to go looking for a stim-juice and a snack.

Amanda was somewhere out of sight, probably picking out a stack of busywork for anyone who looked like they weren't being productive. Rick was probably off until after lunch. No one in sight to talk to or miss her if she left. Unfortunately, she wouldn't be able to access her results from outside the bullpen even if she wanted to brave the streets. A hack yesterday meant the system was locked down until the back door was found and closed.

She flipped her screen on again and accessed the video from the protests. Maybe she could identify a few partici-pants and speed it up. Someone was in some back room making up the charges, but that bottleneck wouldn't affect her work.

From the perspective of the drones, the whole thing could have been a party. No violence. Even low-level shoving and arguments were over in a second. The tension she felt in the middle of it passed over her again like a wave. This might be why the bosses didn't call in the troops — unless you were in the middle of it, you couldn't know how volatile it really was.

She overlaid her own recording on the drone images. Now with an audio track, the crowd became more menacing, but was still smaller than she remembered. The drone footage continued past the end of the audio. Within a half hour of Sofie leaving, the edges of the protests frayed as people reported for shift. Then the rest dispersed.

The order to be prepared for unrest seemed overkill now. People hadn't rioted on the Mallet for decades. Historically, only one uprising had made any difference. In the very early days of the Mallet, the station had been run by commercial interests. The conditions had been brutal even by today's standards. A small group of people led a short coup. Now the descendants of that group were the Elite families. The corporations using the services still ran the Mallet, like any powerful client, but the Elites were local, and the contract stated they were in charge. The people were still living and working in brutal conditions, but no leader had managed to overturn the current structure in the years since.

Sofie recognized three people at the edges of the action and added their names to the interview list. It was unlikely anything would happen to them unless they actually organized the protest.

She checked the progress of her queries. Still a half hour to go, but her request was in the queue, so she had hope.

Nothing from Bindes yet.

The official records would be overloaded for hours, but the open information network held more than just media, conspiracies, and ads. The problem with her meds wasn't unique. Bindes had said remedies for other conditions were showing the same loss of effectiveness. It would be easier to investigate if she knew more about the range of conditions endemic to the Mallet.

She found a site that listed every known chronic condition affecting humans. Way too much information, but she was able to narrow it down to those only found in space. There were six main types of conditions, each with a variety of strains. It was hard for her to believe there was even one healthy person on the Mallet when she finished reading.

"Do you have your reports up-to-date?" Amanda's voice broke Sofie's concentration.

If you didn't keep interrupting me, I'd have them done. Sofie was glad she kept the thought inside because it wasn't fair; Amanda had left her alone for a while.

"By end of day," Sofie said, switching her screen to the report interface. "I was just tracking some of the protest investigation."

"I checked on Rick's progress," Amanda said. "He'll pass his training and be back within the hour. I need a team to be ready for anything that comes from the mess this morning."

Amanda strode off toward Llewelyn's office without letting Sofie make a comment.

Sofie checked the list of reports for her attention. It wouldn't take more than a half hour to complete it. First, she wanted to get through her research and take a quick look at the results of her search.

She pulled a list of the normal medications for Mallet diseases. Most had some kind of permanent surgical solution, but the medications were the cheapest treatment. Some of the operations were so expensive that only a senior Elite would be a candidate.

Her query result arrived, and she merged the data to her open file. Now she could look at it off-line.

The bullpen was still quiet. Sofie didn't want Amanda getting nosy about what she'd been doing instead of filing reports. Her ability to handle the woman without lashing out was getting strained. So, she worked through her list of outstanding reports, and then checked Rick's. He was so far behind she had no hope of covering for him. Instead, she left the bullpen and checked out the snack vendor in the cafeteria. She flashed her credit and punched the keys for the healthiest of the bad-for-you items, synthetic fruit, simulated protein, and vitamin-enhanced chips.

5

R ick strutted back into the bullpen. "Passed. I'm
now certified to put on armor and threaten citi-
zens on a moment's notice."

"Yeah, great that you passed something we all managed
on day one."

He leaned over her shoulder and scanned her screen.
"Don't belittle my accomplishments, please. What's this?"

She told him where she'd gathered the data, but before
Sofie could tell him her ideas, Amanda arrived.

"I have a case for you," she said.

"You don't assign work to us," Sofie said. "Or have you
killed off Llewelyn so you can take charge?"

"Yeah, I haven't seen him since you took over the job."
Rick looked past Amanda to the captain's office. "Maybe we
should go in and make sure there's a live body sitting in the
office."

"Funny," Amanda said, her tone indicating she was less
than amused. "He's in meetings about this unrest. Go ahead
and bother him, see what you get."

It explained the privacy setting on his office, Sofie thought. "Okay, fine, what is it?"

"I know you were looking at the callouts," Amanda said. "It's gone from an annoying inconvenience to a criminal case. Too many people getting sick for it to be coincidence."

She hit something on her pad and both Sofie's and Rick's pads chimed.

"The link to all the records," Amanda said. "It's not just people we've checked for malingering."

No, but is it the first time anyone noticed? "Any theories?" Sofie asked. "We'll need more than the medical records."

"You'll need to interview the doctors and the victims. They are all in a Support clinic. I've sent you the contact information. We've checked and there's no record of it happening before."

"That's no guarantee," Rick said as he hit the link. "This kind of stuff gets purged all the time."

"But we don't think it's a new disease?" Sofie asked. "I mean, we aren't headed for quarantine?"

Quarantine on any space station meant hardship. On the Mallet, it meant death. With no supplies coming in or profits flowing, there would be even more restrictions on food and medicine. If there was no work, the unrest would spread unchecked. But allowing a new disease to leave the station would mean worse. Loss of contracts, isolation. The Elites would be able to get out, but the rest of the population would be left to fight over the dwindling supplies.

"We need to know as soon as possible." Amanda looked around the bullpen. "Keep it confidential. Reports come to me or Llewelyn if he's available."

So now I report to you?

"Okay. But the doctors haven't raised the alarm, right?"

Rick asked. "I'm not feeling great about going into an infection zone."

Amanda sighed. "Look, there's no indication anything is infectious. That won't stop the rumors if we don't keep the news from getting to the public before we have answers. If you jumped to the conclusion of quarantine, it won't take much for anyone else to do the same."

"And when they do, it'll be much harder to stop the rumors." Sofie grabbed her own pad and hit the link. "Fine. Do the doctors know we're coming?"

"The right people have been informed," Amanda said. "I have to get back to the office. I need a report by the end of the day." She left before Sofie could argue about who was in charge.

"If everyone is in one clinic, we won't waste time," Rick said.

"Does it say when that happened? I don't see Maintenance or Manufacturing staff being sent to the same clinic as Support or Admin."

He looked up from his pad. "How did you know there were more than just the frontline workers?"

Sofie laughed. "Amanda said it's not just the malingerers, right? Who else would get away with being sick and not be reported?"

The Admin and Support residents were trusted to get their work done without a lot of supervision. Unlike the workers in Maintenance or Manufacturing, Support residents were not just cogs in a machine that would fail if someone didn't show up.

"What's it like outside now?" Sofie asked. "Any crowds between here and the clinic?"

"It's clear everywhere at the moment," Rick said. "You want to make an appointment with the main doctor?"

And give them time to get their story worked out? "Let's have a look at the info Amanda sent and then drop by. I'd like to see how they react to surprises."

A message came through from Amanda. *You have room zeta, all privacy levels active.*

Room zeta was the smallest case room. "I assume that means her as well as you and me," Sofie said.

"Yeah. No way Amanda would be cut out of the action." Rick stood. "We'll make sure nothing is left lying around for her to spy on."

A case room would make it easier to keep their theories to themselves. Amanda would be suspicious if there was nothing for her to snoop through, but Sofie didn't plan to waste time deciding what tidbits would satisfy her without putting her in their way.

"I doubt it will keep her out of the case, but I like the idea of her being suspicious without cause. Let's get started."

In the room, Sofie turned on the privacy screening then connected her pad to the wall screen. "So, it looks like an even split between the upper and lower levels," she said when the list of people and positions was displayed. "No Elite, no Executive, but they keep pretty separate."

Rick tapped the list of medical concerns to bring it forward. "All have some kind of chronic illness — not the same one. No consistency in the symptoms, unless I'm missing something."

"We can ask the doctors about that. You think maybe it's just a progression of their conditions?" Sofie was careful not to sound too informed on medical issues because most inhabitants of the Mallet didn't know about medications and conditions that needed them. But if more chronic conditions started deteriorating, the case was going to get bigger than a two-person team could handle.

Rick tapped on the list of medications. "See any in common?"

Sofie scanned the list. "Unless the same med has more than one name, I don't think so. But that's not a clue, is it? I mean, medication is pretty tailored to the condition and balanced out for the specific patient."

Rick turned the projection off and handed Sofie her pad back. "I guess we'll find out."

6

The streets were much quieter in the Support section. The closer you got to what people called the front of the Mallet, the cleaner and gentler it got. Despite the difference between sections, the reality of life in a place like the Mallet was that a catastrophe didn't discriminate. That's why unrest was handled carefully. A riot could damage something integral. If the station failed, it killed Elites the same way as the lowliest of Manufacturing workers. Quarantine was supposed to work the same way, but with notice of an outbreak, the Elites would flee.

The clinic was only a ten-minute walk from the police station. Sofie didn't come to the section enough to know whether the traffic was normal. But the clinic sign shone a warm and welcoming green. Calming music drifted out when she reached the entrance. Inside, everything looked clean, but smelled of fresh air and something treelike rather than the disinfectant she expected.

"Makes me wish I needed a bit of attention," Rick said. "Who would want to leave?"

"You have no idea how boring it is. People constantly

checking your vitals. No clocks, so you aren't ever sure whether you should be asleep or awake."

He turned to her. "You spend a lot of time in a clinic?"

She hoped the answer would always be the same to that kind of question. If the operation was successful, she wouldn't ever have to come into a place like this again. "My mother was a nurse. I came after school when I was a kid. She made sure I did my homework, and I watched the patients float in a kind of suspension. I got to leave every day. Most of them were in for a week or two."

"Nice to have a mom who cared," Rick said. "Most kids grew up like me. Parents too busy or worn out to oversee anything."

That was the only good part of growing up on the Mallet, Sofie thought. Your future wasn't tied to your parents' status. Schooling sorted the Manufacturing and Maintenance from the Support and Authority workers — sometimes the scale got tipped for a price, of course. Executive and Elite were the exceptions. You had to be born into those sections, or in the very rare case, find a way to buy yourself in.

The receptionist greeted them and offered stim-juice and comfortable chairs. "Doctor Starlight with be with you in a moment," he said. "She will escort you to the ward."

"I'm already here, Rupert." The speaker was a short woman with wiry black hair and a grin. "Come with me. I'll get you set up and we can discuss what you are going to do while you're here."

Rick prepared to follow the doctor, but Sofie remained where she was. "Doctor Starlight, I think you might be under the wrong impression."

"Oh, call me Petra," the woman said. "You are here to interview my patients, is that right?"

"Yes, and we will decide what we ask," Sofie said. "This is an investigation."

The woman reached for Sofie's elbow and drew her forward. "Yes, yes. I didn't mean I was going to tell you how to do your job. I meant I was going to tell you how I do mine. These are sick people, and I need to ensure they are not made worse by the experience."

Sofie didn't resist the small tug on her arm. The doctor gave her nothing to resist, anyway. Their conversation would be better held out of the public areas if Sofie needed to insist on having her way.

Petra led them past a ward of patients toward a cubicle. About half of the beds contained sleeping bodies, and the rest stared listlessly as she walked by. There were two nurses checking machines attached to the arms of unconscious patients.

In the cubicle, the doctor pointed to two chairs. "Have a seat and I'll put on the white noise, so we won't be over-heard." When Sofie remained standing, Petra said, "It doesn't extend very far beyond the walls of the cube. Please, sit and we'll be finished soon."

Rick rolled his eyes at her then patted the seat. He was right. She was being obstructive because of her childhood and her fears about the upcoming procedure.

She sat and leaned forward. "We aren't here to upset anyone. We need to know as much as we can about the situation so we can recommend actions."

"I can give you most of what you need," Petra said. "I am the only doctor assigned to the case, so the treatments are controlled. What are your questions? I'll put together a report for you on anything that will help."

Why is she trying to keep us away from the patients? Sofie tried not to read anything into the woman's actions. Most of the doctors she'd met as a child really cared about making people well.

"We need to know how they ended up here," Rick said. "I mean, this is a Support clinic, right? More than half of the people in those beds are Maintenance or Manufacturing. So why are they here?"

"Trends worry us," Petra said. "I requested the people affected by this... whatever it is, be brought together. Minimize the risk if this is contagious. Also, as I said, it gives them consistent care. That should help you as well."

"Is there any chance we're looking at a new disease?" Sofie asked. There were no precautions in place in the ward, so she'd be surprised if the answer was yes. She hoped that it was no, but hope didn't live long in her job.

"We can't rule it out completely, but I don't think so. Or if it is, the transmission rate is very low. The important variable is that everyone here has an underlying condition. Different ones, but still, none of them are completely healthy."

"Are they suffering from the underlying conditions?" Sofie asked. "Did they stop taking treatment?"

One of the nurses hurried by and Petra scanned the ward. Sofie did the same, but there was no indication that anyone was suddenly worse.

"No," Petra answered. "Well, I suppose that's not completely true. None admit to skipping the medications. Some of them are showing the expected symptoms and we've boosted their dosage, hoping they respond. But others are presenting different symptoms from what we expect."

"We still need to interview people," Sofie said. "But I apologize for my attitude earlier. You've been helpful. Can we get the medical records of their treatment here?"

"Of course," Petra said. "I'll have someone send them

along if you tell me where. There is one more thing. One more commonality. All the patients reported feeling a little unwell and then waking up feeling much, much worse. That's an unusual progression."

Rick gave Petra a link to send the documents. Sofie and Rick split the conscious patients between them. The interviews were brief, confirming Petra's report and adding nothing new.

7

"I'll meet you back at the case room," Sofie said at the point where she needed to turn off for The Open Pit. "I want to check something with a contact."

"Your contact for those pills you're dropping?" Rick asked.

Sofie wanted to tell him, but the operation would be done soon. Then maybe when it wasn't a problem any longer, she'd tell him about the Fades. It was better that he think she had a drug problem than know the truth. Drugs taken off duty were not a problem for any cop's career. A hidden genetic condition that could put her fellow officers at risk was more than a problem.

"Someone who could have a different take on this information," she said. "You really want to take one doctor's view? Someone who might have a reason to lie to us?"

"Fine, you keep your secrets, I'll keep mine," he said.

"You don't have any secrets," Sofie said, chuckling. "We all know everyone you sleep with or want to sleep with."

"Sex isn't the only thing in my life," he said in mock offense. "Maybe I'm a secret plant from internal affairs?"

"Sure. Let's go with that. Seriously, I'm not ready to introduce you to my contact. I won't be long, and I might get some answers."

He gave her a mocking bow and headed toward the case room.

Sofie watched him cross the bullpen before she started moving toward the bar to meet with Bindes. Rick wouldn't follow her. Or would he? The man was a great partner, but he did have an itch to find out her secrets.

She sent a message to Bindes to prevent a long wait when she arrived at the bar. He didn't respond, but that wasn't unusual.

When she walked through the door, Sofie automatically scanned the room. As usual, it was quiet at this time of day. A few drinkers sat on stools facing the bartender. Three tables were occupied by tired looking workers. The booth that served as Bindes's consulting room was empty.

She walked up and got the attention of the bartender. Today it was a woman with an easy smile that was probably meant to set people at ease.

"You know where Bindes is?" Sofie asked. She didn't have the time or the appetite for small talk.

"Went into the back a couple of hours ago," the woman said. "Guessing it's for a hit of VR."

Bindes was addicted to the drug. It was the other side of the deal he made with Sofie for her treatments. She got the meds; he got a blind eye turned to his drug usage. It wasn't the kind of thing that would affect his performance, so Sofie didn't get many pangs of conscience over it, but VR was still one of the few illegal drugs. If he'd been under for a couple of hours, the experience was about to end. He'd be disoriented, but that would pass fast.

"You have a key?" Sofie asked.

"No. Only Bindes has that," the woman said. "I'll buzz him. That's the best I can do. He'll come out when he's ready."

"I'll wait for a bit," Sofie said. Bindes's opinion was important, but she could come back later if needed. She ordered a stim-juice and settled in her usual place. If Bindes wasn't out by the time she finished, she'd leave.

The door to his small office opened by the time Sofie had drunk half of her stim-juice. Bindes blinked a few times at the brightness of the lighting and then focused on her. He touched the wall and steadied himself for a moment. VR was best experienced in a completely dark room, and it left the user with vertigo. Sofie never saw the attraction. Real life waited for you when you came down, so why bother?

Bindes motioned to the bartender. She drew a pint of beer and sent it to the table.

"Sofie, good to see you again. Bit surprising, but good." Bindes drew a long sip from the glass.

"I thought you were keeping your trips to your off-duty time."

"I don't have any of that, do I?" Bindes asked. "Between here and the few hours I work at the legit clinics, I'm always working."

"Clearly not always. How long were you under?" If it had been more than a couple of hours, he'd be useless for critical thinking.

"A short trip this time. A beautiful beach on old Earth. Before the fall. Although I guess we only have the history books to tell us what that means. The rest of the time I was making plans for our little date."

"Okay. Thanks." Sofie pulled out her pad. "Are you able to think straight?"

"As straight as usual," Bindes said. "What do you need?"

Sofie told him about the visit to the clinic. "I need a second medical assessment of the data."

"Which doctor?" Bindes reached for her pad to read the notes.

"Petra Starlight."

"She's good at her job. A bit too trusting of her patients, but you can rely on what she tells you. She's less likely to pass on guesses, so you need to press her if you need speculation."

Sofie waited while Bindes scanned the information. The bar started to fill up, as though people knew the doctor was back on the job.

"Okay. You think it's like your meds, right?"

"Yes, but I hope it's not. If we're facing widespread medical fraud, we're screwed. Even if we stop it, people won't have confidence in the system anymore."

He nodded distractedly, still reading through the medical records. "Hmm. I think Petra must know it's not a coincidence. But she's like you, not ready to face the consequences if she's right."

"Is that it?" Sofie asked.

He passed her pad back. "If you send me more information, I can do a bit of digging. But you need to decide whether it's worth the risk of someone finding out."

Finding out that she'd shared information? Probably easy to hide that action. Finding out she was working with a semi-disgraced doctor with a VR addiction? It wouldn't take long for even an incompetent investigator to find the truth.

"How about we keep it off-line," she said. "Grab something and write down what you need."

8

S ofie headed back to the case room to start checking on the backgrounds of the patients, Petra Starlight, and the various meds. The corridors of the Maintenance section were busy, but nothing felt out of the ordinary. No one muttering in a corner, not even a small crowd. She didn't trust this peace so soon after the problems earlier, but maybe the ringleaders were in custody, and no one was worked up enough to start again — yet.

The case room was dark from the outside. Good. Her side research wouldn't be seen by anyone. Her gut said there was a connection between the illnesses and her meds failing, but she had nothing to prove it. And a little voice in the dark part of her mind said she wanted there to be a link so badly she was making it happen. Corruption on the Mallet was so widespread everyone had their fingers in some kind of illicit pie. And there was no guarantee it wasn't two separate schemes: slowing down production by keeping workers too ill to report for shift, and skimming for profit.

She flashed her pass at the door and slipped inside. Rick was there talking to someone on the pad — hopefully a contact giving them a lead. His flirting didn't mean the call wasn't professional. They both knew it was an effective tool for convincing people to talk. He nodded to her and kept going. Sofie pulled out her pad and projected the data on the wall.

A list of conditions, and the medications that managed the symptoms. A list of names attached to conditions. She started compiling questions as they came to her. Did the patient change their dosage? Were the prescriptions filled recently? Any new dispensaries? Part of her itched to add her own details. Condition: Fades. No prescription. Dosage increased drastically.

What if the patients they knew about were only the worst cases and more people were just hanging on at work? Or how many residents of the Mallet were like her, hiding a condition with black market meds?

"I've talked to a few of the family members," Rick said. "Not sure if they were any help. I mean, who has time to check on someone who should have the sense to reach out if they're in trouble?"

Sofie typed her question on the notes document. "I've got someone looking into background. This is going to be a hard one to get a handle on."

"We'll find something," Rick said. "Maybe it's all a coincidence and we'll be onto a nice, juicy murder soon."

The door to the case room opened and Amanda stepped inside. "How did your meeting with the doctors go?"

Sofie tensed. If Amanda took interest and found a connection to the Fades, she was fucked. "I thought we had tight security on this room." Maybe starting on the offensive would make her back off.

"I have access to all the rooms," Amanda said. "Do you

have secrets you don't want me to know about?" She said it with a laugh, but Sofie saw through the act.

"You know how it is," Rick said. "A case brings lots of false leads. You never liked anyone driving from behind on your investigations."

He's trying to protect me because he thinks I'm taking drugs. Or maybe he's just trying to stop me shooting my mouth off and causing problems. Sofie wondered if Rick could be trusted with the truth. But it wouldn't be a thing for much longer. So let him think what he wanted.

"Do you have any leads?" Amanda glanced at the wall. "There's pressure to divert resources."

"There's always pressure," Sofie said. "We have a lot of data and it's leading to more questions. That's pretty normal a few hours into any case."

"It's also a way to waste time. Keep focused, Sofie. If this is a crime, solve it fast, and if it's not, close it."

"What pressure?" Rick asked.

Protecting her again. This time it was familiar. Sofie swallowed her reaction to Amanda. *She knows you are a good detective. Just because you hear a putdown doesn't mean it is one.* Rick said it often enough that Sofie turned it into a mantra. Amanda was also a good detective. Her career ambitions didn't make her a bad person.

"This morning. The Elite families are reaching out through their aides. They want to be sure it's not going to turn into something more."

"You mean they want enough notice to get away before it turns violent," Sofie said before Rick could intervene.

Would the Mallet be a better place without the Elites for a while?

"Not only the violence," Amanda said. "If there's a disease."

The Elites would all have planet-side refuges. Places they could ride out a quarantine without spreading the infection across the local system. A nice mountain compound, or a private island, or both.

"Why do they stay?" Sofie asked. "I mean, they could run their businesses from anywhere. The Mallet isn't a great place to live, even up in the Elite section."

"Like we can understand what drives an Elite," Rick said.

"Power," Amanda said. "On the Mallet, they are rulers. Planet-side, just another bunch of rich assholes. And maybe there's something in the contract? I don't have time to waste poking into something I can't affect."

If I had enough credit, I'd live in a place that wasn't likely to blow up if something went wrong. "I guess. So, anything else, or can we get back to picking through this stuff?" Sofie nodded to the data on the wall.

Amanda glanced at the projection long enough that Sofie expected her to point out the connections no one else could see. Or ask for it all to be sent to her. If Amanda found the link, Sofie would be fine with it; data analysis was her strength anyway.

"No. Just focus on what relates to the case," she said. "I know the missing kids helped us with the Sato murder, but not every bit of peripheral data is linked."

"But sometimes it is," Sofie couldn't stop herself from saying. "You're good at analyzing data, why don't you stick around?"

Amanda looked at the lists again and then shook her head. "I'm too busy with my new job. You need to be ready to protect the station if the protests start up again."

"Yes," Rick said. "You said that already. I passed the assessment. Sofie has her gear upgraded. Just let us know when and where."

When the door shut behind Amanda, Rick pulled up a chair to face the wall. "Okay, where were we?"

"It doesn't bother you? Her coming in when she wants?"

He shrugged. "Yeah, but there's nothing we can do about it. Just the same as last time. What we don't want her to see, we keep out of the room."

9

___

Sofie's vision blurred. She blinked and the numbers on the wall cleared. Not a symptom of the Fades, but definitely one of staring too long at the same data. She couldn't make sense of anything. Rick had given up an hour ago and gone to talk to his contacts. Or eat, or have a quick date with a friend.

Bindes hadn't called with any new information or directions through the medical labyrinth. It was time to take a different tack, and it was not going to include the spreadsheet on the wall.

"It's not a case yet," she murmured. That could be the biggest problem. She was looking to solve what might just be a coincidence.

She could head to the clinic and talk to Petra, but what about? Again, until she was sure there was a crime, she had no focus for any questions. At least she'd get out of this room if she headed for the Support section. Her mind needed stimulation, or at the very least a different view.

Sofie closed the projection and tucked her pad into a

pocket. Case or not, she liked to surprise people, so no heads-up call to Petra. The bullpen was empty when she stepped through the case room door. She couldn't remember a time when it had been deserted like this. She glanced at the newsfeed screen; everything looked peaceful still. She shrugged and told herself it had nothing to do with her case.

She glanced over at Llewelyn's office. She could see the back of Amanda's head. Her hair was sculpted into a wedge of black curls, making her look even taller. Llewelyn sat across from her. Neither was acting like there was an urgent problem that had pulled everyone out of the office. She headed out toward the clinic in the Support section, telling herself she was close enough to return if they needed her urgently.

There were more people on the street than earlier, and they weren't hustling from one important meeting to another. Or even pretending to be busy. Sofie took in the faces as she walked. The pedestrians were tired, and a few carried scars on cheeks and foreheads. They were not Support residents. A closer glance showed their clothes were ill-fitting and worn. If the protests here were triggered by infiltrators, they would have no way of containing the unrest within Maintenance. Trying to arrest or use the normal control methods on a crowd of Support staff, even if they were imposters, would create a media storm about safety and respect, and whatever else would stir up subscribers. Someone had found a new way to cause trouble.

She opened her pad and typed a message to Llewelyn. *Looks like Maintenance residents are planning something in Support.* She took a few images of the frayed clothing, not turning the camera to faces so no one noticed.

The clinic was only a few more corridors along. Sofie kept walking while she waited for acknowledgment.

The building had the same caring hush as before. Everything designed to create a feeling of safety and healing. The receptionist sent her back to the ward after verifying Petra was still on duty.

"Have you found anything?" the doctor asked as she came forward to greet Sofie. "The patients are still stable."

Sofie scanned the room before suggesting they talk in Petra's cubicle. She suspected that a few of the patients were feigning sleep, maybe to avoid the attention of the nurses, or to overhear any valuable gossip they could sell.

When they were seated with stim-juice cups on the desk, Sofie shared her frustration with the data.

Petra chuckled. "I remember that feeling as a student. What can I do to help?"

"If someone is causing this, how would they do it? I mean there are all kinds of conditions and more treatments than illnesses. As far as I've worked out, one condition can have several options for treatment, and it depends on the patient. And others have only one option to manage the symptoms."

Petra pulled out her pad and flicked through some screens before answering. "Ah, here it is. You are right, but that's not the complete picture. Some of what you see as different medications are the same medicine with different brand names. Separate naming helps to keep records of which section of the Mallet requires more or less attention."

And the meds can be made more cheaply for the lower castes. Was that the underlying crime? Weaker meds for the workers? No, that made no sense since low production meant low profits. "Has it helped?" she asked.

"Oh yes. We often find that the Temporaries have

brought in a new problem despite the sanitization protocols. We usually contain it before it leaves the immediate area. An increase in the need for genetic condition treatments in an area can mean a problem with the life-support system."

Having the different brand names for the same treatment gave them a faster indicator than noticing an uptick in clinic visits and then figuring out exactly where it was happening. It made sense, but Sofie wondered if that was the best way to monitor the life-support systems. Genetic conditions would take generations to develop.

"Are the medications manufactured the same way?" It would help if she didn't have to track through shadow production lines. Pharmaceuticals came from the Support labs and farms; if each one had a different path to distribution, she'd never get through it with only Rick to help.

"A number of the medications are manufactured off-station. There are inspectors to ensure the quality standards are met for what we manufacture, but that's all I know. Are you thinking someone is messing with the meds going to Maintenance? I have patients from Admin and Support here."

But no Executive or Elite.

"I'm just grasping at anything that might help the case." Sofie felt her pad buzz, but she ignored it. The message could wait a few more minutes.

"Would it help if I gave you the matrix of brands?" Petra asked. "That's how we prescribe. All doctors from the Elite to the lowest level of Manufacturing know the clinical names of the correct treatments, and we prescribe by level."

And almost every clinic treated people across the castes, providing initial medical attention before triaging the patient to the correct clinic.

"That would help, thanks." She didn't look forward to

more hours sitting in front of a screen trying to find a pattern.

Petra sent the document to Sofie's pad. "Anything else I can do to help?"

"You're more likely to know the answer to that than me," Sofie said. "Where would you look?"

"I assume you look for motive," Petra said. "But I suppose I would be talking to the quality inspectors, or, since I have some background in lab work, I'd go observe. But I'm not police. I would be looking for a way to cure my patients, not to arrest a criminal."

Sofie thanked her. As Petra walked her to the exit, she checked the patients, hoping someone would wake and talk to her. The ward seemed more crowded than before. "Are there more people here?"

"Yes, four more. I haven't had a chance to delve into their histories, but I'll send you the details and records as soon as I have anything."

The crowds of impostors were gone when she walked back to the bullpen. Sofie checked the message she'd ignored before. Llewelyn. *Infiltrators taken care of. Good catch.* She hoped he was right.

Another message came through as she read Llewelyn's. Nhu Eckerman, the Executive liaison for the Elite Ruiz family, was demanding a meeting.

10

When an Executive made demands, the only sensible choice was to obey. Nhu's message included a link to their meeting space and an appointment time five minutes from now.

Sofie wouldn't be able to get back to the case room in time, and she needed some semblance of privacy on her side of the video. The clinic sat next to a quiet stim-juice stand, one with tables and booths inside. Sofie ordered a Rellian blufroot flavored stim-juice and sat at the back of a half-moon booth as far from any other table as she could manage. She dug into her pocket for her earpiece and connected to the meeting space. It was functional and bland, the only decoration an empty glass vase. Nhu, who was divided gender, was masculine today. The meeting would be short and to the point.

Nhu appeared, sitting in a black office chair, two minutes after the set time. They were outfitted in a sleek gray suit and bright blue blouse.

"Thank you for being prompt," they said. "This concerns the events of this morning."

Sofie nodded. "The unrest?" No way was Nhu interested in some sick Maintenance workers.

"A little more than that. The Prathams held a meeting to agree on the right approach in resolving this... problem. The Ruiz family volunteered to communicate the information to the appropriate individuals."

Was she supposed to be grateful to be on the list? "I see. And what can I do to assist you?"

Nhu smiled as though they believed her humble attitude. "I understand you are investigating this mysterious ailment."

"Yes, Rick and I are working to find out if this is a crime or a coincidence."

"Neither the Pratham nor I are interested in who is assisting you. We do not think that a finding of coincidence will resolve the conflict. It is our opinion that you must find that a crime has been committed and arrest the criminal responsible. The rabble-rousers must be satisfied with your result."

Meaning they didn't care about the truth — no surprise there — and they wanted a fast resolution. Sofie didn't agree that a handpicked scapegoat would work. If the lie was exposed, it would ignite the protest leaders and cause the very situation that the Elites were trying to avoid.

"Do they have a fall guy picked out?" she asked.

"There is no need for your sarcasm, Detective." Nhu glanced at something off-screen, shook their head, and turned back to Sofie. "I'm sure you understand that sometimes a manufactured outcome is the optimal choice."

Nhu might not know all the details of her last case, but clearly they suspected she'd made up the facts that closed the investigation into the murder of the Sato Pratham. Or perhaps they did more than suspect it. If they knew the truth about Oswald Sato and the Ruiz Pratham's business arrangements, they would know Sofie'd lied. This was her least favorite aspect of Nhu's genders. Underneath the veneer they were both conniving and manipulative, but the female Nhu took the time to stroke her ego. Not that it made a difference in the end, but it felt nicer.

"I was serious," Sofie said. "I can work faster if I know the full instructions. If there is a scapegoat with a plausible motive, please inform me now."

There was silence.

I should have remembered to keep my mouth shut.

"No. The Prathams believe that is your job. What is the status of your investigation at the moment? Perhaps I can offer some perspective."

That was a line Sofie wouldn't cross. The moment she handed over details of an investigation, she handed over any shred of control.

"The investigation is moving along. I thank you for your offer, but I will continue as I have in the past. My success rate is high enough that I am given leeway."

"Yes. You've used that wisely up to now."

Sofie's knee started bouncing in frustration under the table. In theory this kind of pressure was supposed to trickle down from the captain after being strained through his experience and practicality. Nhu didn't know or care how Sofie worked. It was enough of a change from their normal approach that Sofie wondered if she was missing some subtext.

"When you say that the Prathams agreed that the Ruiz Pratham would communicate the desired outcome, does that mean I won't hear from anyone else? That you are my sole contact?"

Nhu nodded to someone off-screen. "That was the

agreement. I make no comment on the reliability of other families to follow through on their commitment."

So Haadiya, the Sato liaison, would be calling in on them at some point. "Am I expected to report if anyone contacts me?"

Nhu smiled this time and Sofie saw a hint of their softer side. They were amused, so there would probably be no repercussions for her questions. "I have no power over the other Executive liaisons. If you wish to give me leverage by reporting on their activities, that is up to you."

"One more question, if I may?"

"One more and no more. I am expected by my Pratham. To report on this meeting, amongst other things."

"Is there a deadline? This type of thing takes time. Finding evidence of a crime, then the clues pointing to a suspect. If it does turn out to be someone tampering with medical treatment, or some other way of making people ill, I don't have to work so hard to prove it. But I would like to know when I must have a result."

"Hours before the current agitation becomes a crisis."

Sofie's screen went black as Nhu ended the meeting.

11

R   ick was in the case room when Sofie slipped
        through the door. He was making notes on his
        pad while staring at the wall of data.

"I have more to add," Sofie said. "Maybe we'll find some clarity?"

"Having more information will eventually shine a light, but I'm sick of trying to make sense of all this stuff." He tossed his pad on the table and showed her the notes. The writing was barely legible. She saw names, some of them belonging to Elite families.

"What is this?"

"What did you find?" he asked instead of answering her.

"I got told by Nhu we need to solve this case or risk being blamed for the ensuing riots. And I have the clinical names of the drugs along with the reason they have different dispensing names, and some ideas on more people to interview."

"Maybe that will help us make some progress. I got the records of people with the conditions," he said. "Trying to see if we're about to be deluged with sick people."

Sofie reached for his pad and scrolled through a long list of conditions, each with a number listed beside it. Those she could make out were enough to form an ice ball in her gut. "Too many," she whispered. "This has to run across castes. It's ten or maybe twenty percent of the population."

"Yeah. Someone should be looking into why so many people are kept alive with drugs. This can't be a coincidence. The Mallet is killing people."

"That's not new." She scrolled again. "We need to add this to the database. Do you have the castes of all these patients? And their names?"

"My contact is sending it all along. I took a few notes to get me started. But this isn't all of it. If there's something wrong with the medications, or if whatever caused the conditions is increasing, riots are the last thing we need to worry about."

We can't do much about the environment of the Mallet. "There's a crime in here somewhere. Let's hope it's one we can handle. And do it fast."

The door opened and Amanda stepped through. "Progress?"

"When has a case moved fast at this stage?" Rick asked. "We have more data, and it's definitely a crime. We just need to figure out what to call it, and whether it's one corrupt asshole putting people in danger, or someone trying to cover up a murder with excess bodies that are currently still clinging to life. Or if it's station-wide and can't be stopped."

"I've been contacted by five of the Elite families through various intermediaries," Amanda said.

"Let me guess. If we don't find a way to explain that this is just people getting sick and will not get worse and is no one's fault, then we're responsible for any riots." Sofie reached over and turned off the projector.

"Just about," Amanda said. "The problem is they're right. We need to solve the case in a way that calms people down."

"No," Sofie said. "We solve cases. We don't pick an outcome. That's all about the hype afterwards. Our job is to catch the criminal, your job is to communicate the results in a way that accomplishes whatever goal the Elites have."

It was a rare case that changed her mind about her job. Sofie couldn't repeat what she'd done, what all three of them had done, in the Sato murder investigation. In that case, the man they pinned it on was already dead, and he'd been the kind of asshole who bought and sold kids when he was alive. Making a decision about who gets punished and who goes free was a fast road to vigilante justice. Vigilantes were never the good guys.

"Just give me something I can use to calm people down." Amanda glanced at the blank wall and then down to Rick's pad. "I can help with data analysis if you ask."

"Stick with your new duties," Sofie said. "We've got this."

Amanda left without another offer.

"So, what happened to her being too busy to help?" Sofie shrugged off her jacket and settled in.

"Priorities change." Rick turned on the projector and swiveled his chair to face the wall. "Let her do her thing while we solve the case."

"It feels like we're doing her thing right now," Sofie said. "If this was a normal investigation, Amanda would be picking through data and finding us a clue to follow."

Sofie added the clinical names of the drugs and sorted the information so they could see patterns.

"Helping Llewelyn will help us," Rick said. "This is interesting. Do we have any information on the supply chain for meds?"

"It should be accessible," Sofie said, entering the request. "Yeah. Ten minutes."

Rick's pad pinged. "The full list of people with these conditions." He projected the file onto a blank space as a hierarchy of castes. "Looks like it follows the usual spread of population. Nothing to suggest that anyone is targeting a specific group or condition."

The new display was a pyramid rather than a bar chart. A few Elites from different families, a few more Executives, and so on down to the wide base of the Manufacturing and Maintenance names.

"Can you display it by condition?" Sofie asked. "Maybe it's not by caste, but by medication."

The resulting graph showed a fairly equal spread across the medications.

"Okay, I'm ready to open a case file," Sofie said. "Tampering with medication causing harm. Does that work for you?"

"Do we celebrate step one?" Rick asked. "I mean, it's taken us less than a day to find a crime. Who knows, we might have a perpetrator before end of shift."

"Why don't you go get some junk food and stim-juice while I do the paperwork."

When she was alone, Sofie took her meds out and looked at the brand name. Bindes was getting his free meds from a Support clinic. His contact there might have answers. And just maybe, if they solved the problem with the meds, she wouldn't have to get the operation.

Petra's message came through as Sofie submitted the case documentation. An attached file included the names of people who signed off on the meds ordered by the clinic. A quick scan showed three names listed more often than the others. Anna Kivi, Deva Lu, and Selma Gold. She added the file to their research bucket and started looking into these people. When her request for the supply chain details came through, those names would be the way in.

12

S ofie stared at the new information on the wall. The process for testing and distributing the meds spread across the entire surface as a series of steps. The previous month's numbers for the meds they'd targeted were displayed at every step where volume was checked. She'd highlighted the points where Kivi, Lu, or Gold were involved. It looked like Kivi was some kind of part-time manager, part-time subordinate. She received fifty percent of the incoming shipments. She signed off on the reconciliation after the meds were assigned their caste-specific brand names. She also authorized most of the shipments to clinics.

"Do you see anything that might point to skimming, or tampering?" she asked Rick.

He walked along the wall, occasionally reaching out to expand a section. Sofie didn't interrupt. Mainly because she had no idea what he was looking for. The key touch points were assigned to multiple people. As far as she could see, no one of the three people followed a shipment from receiving point to distribution. Collusion was possible, but when more than one person was involved in a plot, the risk of discovery was so much higher.

"No real skimming," Rick said as he ended his survey of the steps. "There are a few minimal percentage differences at the reconciliation points, but not enough to be more than just spillage."

She didn't relish picking through their scant under-standing of the process all day. She couldn't just slip out and go to the Open Pit to ask Bindes for his take. Rick would start asking questions she didn't want to answer if she kept disappearing. "I know someone," she said. "He's a contact, and I have to ask if he's okay with me bringing you along."

"And you don't want me asking awkward questions," Rick said. "Fine. I'll hit the head and meet you at the entrance."

When the door closed behind him, Sofie reached out to Dr. Bindes and explained the situation.

"Don't come here," he said. "I have a reputation as an outlaw to uphold. I'll send you a link to a meeting space and you can show me what you have."

Sofie sent a message to Rick that they weren't leaving. A moment later, the link pinged on her pad, and she opened the meeting space. This one was just a black screen.

"We'll keep this all private," Bindes said, his voice so muffled it took Sofie a moment to recognize it.

"What do I call you?" She appreciated the effort at anonymizing his location and appearance.

"Mr. B. Can you bring the projection in a little? It's hard to see."

Rick stepped in as Sofie placed her pad on a stand facing the wall. "I'll set it to scroll at your command," she said, making the adjustments.

"Give me a few minutes to study it."

Rick joined Sofie at the table, moving one of the chairs next to her. Bindes muttered, "Scroll left, scroll right, scroll up, scroll down," as they waited.

"It's tense outside," Rick said. "I think they're releasing the ringleaders soon."

It was easy to ignore what was happening on the station while she pored over information in the room. "Protests?"

"Not yet. But you can see about forty people hanging around the jail entrance."

"Okay," Bindes said. "There are a few things."

Rick grabbed his pad to take notes. "Go ahead."

A pointer appeared at the first step of the process. "Assuming this is the volume for a month, what we're bringing in looks right. So it's not about a shortage. No one is diluting meds to cover up a drop in supply."

Supply issues hadn't occurred to Sofie. "Any red flags at all?"

"Don't interrupt," Bindes said. "You noticed the discrepancies where the reconciliation between branded and unbranded meds occurred?"

"Yes," Rick said. "It looked within a normal range to me."

"And you know what the normal range is? Then I'm done here." Sofie recognized the fake tone of his sarcasm. Bindes was hooked on finding the answer.

"No," Sofie said. "We don't know, we guess. That's why I called you."

She heard a chuckle. Bindes was playing with Rick.

"It's not that far off normal. But the actual numbers are huge. If you think of it in terms of patients, what you call 'spillage' is around fifty patients' worth of medication."

But the patients were all getting their meds. If someone

was skimming, they still had to dilute the dosage to make the numbers work. "Is there some kind of reconciliation of prescriptions to supply?"

"Yes, and you can probably get it, but it's a lagging indicator. The meds arrive, the doctors prescribe over the subsequent days and weeks. It will be difficult to pinpoint a problem fast enough."

"I'm guessing that's not the reason people are getting sick," Rick said. "Or not the reason for our case, right?"

"Yes, it's not numbers, even if you can rely on the patient prescription records being accurate. It's about dosages, shelf life, and ingredients. The meds are being diluted, or the expiry dates are being manipulated. A medication at full strength will work; most will work less effectively as they reach their expiry date. And that's not when they stop working, just when they become too weak to help much."

"Where could that happen?" Sofie stared at the process steps, but she couldn't see any loops or open-ended flows. "How do meds get taken out of circulation?"

"The dispensaries ship them to a central point for destruction. We burn them. The dispensary will only fill a prescription with meds that have a six-month minimum life. If meds are being switched, it will be at the destruction point, I think. But I don't have the kind of criminal mind to know where someone could build loops into the process. For instance, where a criminal would be able to divert those slated for incineration to the incoming supply."

Was another process they would need to request data on all he had to offer? Although, Sofie admitted it did give them a whole lot of other people to add to the suspect list.

"Is that all?" Sofie asked. "I mean, that was valuable, and if you have more insights, I would love to hear them."

"No. Like I said, I don't think that way."

Sofie thanked Bindes and exited the meeting space.

"So, more processes to study and more people to inter-view." Rick stretched out his shoulders and back.

"We haven't really started interviewing yet," Sofie said. "I think we begin with the three names we found so far."

Sofie checked the contact information for Kivi, Lu, and Gold, then dug out the names of the inspectors for the Mallet-manufactured items. Oddly, there were a few duplicated meds. She made a note to ask why it made sense to import and fabricate the same thing.

"You want to drop in on them now?" Rick asked. "It's pretty late."

It was too early in the case to go hard on interviews. When they had a real suspect, or a few of them, they'd start dragging people in for interrogation. "Tomorrow, early. The three people authorizing the meds for distribution are on shift. If we hit around eight hours in the morning, we should be able to catch them. I found five inspectors. We'll check on them later."

"You think it's the distribution process?" Rick asked. "Maybe a bit of attention will stop the problem until we look away."

Sofie didn't have a lot of confidence in the idea. Greed was a powerful motivator, and usually behind greed was a goal, like buying power. If their perpetrator was close to the final stages of their plan, pressure was more likely to speed them up than stall them. It would be better for the case if the criminal panicked. Criminals were much easier to catch when they made mistakes.

"I'm too tired to think about that," Sofie said. She rolled her shoulders and stretched. "There's nothing urgent for tonight."

Someone rapped on the door. Rick checked the door cam. "Haadiya."

"Nhu is supposed to be the liaison," Sofie said. "Should I call and complain to them that we've had visits interrupting our progress?"

"Yeah, implying Nhu can't control their peers is bound to go well." He checked that every piece of information was put away and released the door lock.

"Evening," Haadiya said, scanning the room. "I haven't been here for a while. I'm sure you've missed me."

Sofie stood and tucked her chair under the table. "Is there something we can help you with?"

Haadiya turned from his search of the blank wall, cleared table, and shut-down pads. "It is regarding the recent unrest."

"Nhu Eckerman informed me that they are our contact for the Elites. Is that not the official stance?" Sofie kept her voice pleasant, hoping to shut him down without offending. An offended Executive could make her life hell.

"Yes, for the official reports," Haadiya said. "But you understand that the murder of the previous Pratham has the Sato family on edge. We are concerned about any... finger-pointing."

Sofie looked over at Rick. Haadiya was his contact in the upper levels. Why wasn't he stepping in? Her partner was glancing at the pad in his hands, skimming headlines.

"We have no indication of any Elite family being involved," she said. "Until a few minutes ago, we were not even sure there was a crime."

"Yes, the sickness." Haadiya waved his hand as though to dismiss it. "I am concerned about these protests."

Sofie thought back to her experience in the crowd. The muttering and chanting were about people being sick. Was Haadiya hinting the two were not connected? It would definitely be easier if that was true. She suspected the sickness was just a trigger for the protests, and solving the problem with the meds would simply make the protesters shift their rhetoric.

Rick looked up from his screen. "We're investigating the increase in clinic admittances. I can find out who's leading the team responsible for managing the protests, if you like."

Haadiya didn't say anything for a moment. Sofie saw the tiny wrinkles at his temples as he thought. If he demanded Rick be reassigned, she would be stuck with some rookie who would argue every step of her investigation hoping to show how smart they were.

"Not necessary," Haadiya said. "I'm sure they are competent at crowd control. I suppose I am under the same impression as the Prathams — should you find nothing untoward in your case, the protests will settle."

"You think we'll find a Pratham involved in the sickness?" Sofie wouldn't be surprised. Nothing to do with profit on the Mallet slipped past an Elite.

"I would never suggest such a thing." Haadiya shuddered. "I worry that the lower castes are determined to blame the Elite families, as they always do. And yes, the unfortunate circumstance of Oswald Sato's demise is just the tinder they look for to spark trouble."

He meant riots, but most people on the Mallet avoided using the word. Like saying it would bring on a disaster.

"We've found nothing to indicate who is involved," Sofie said. "It's too early to point to anyone. If it looks like our case's resolution would cause the Satos problems, then Rick will give you a heads-up."

"Much appreciated."

"Is there a chance we'll find something like that?" Sofie asked. "It would be better if we knew. If you need us to minimize damage, the more informed we are, the better."

Haadiya shrugged and moved to leave. "I am not aware of anything, but, as you know, I'm not privy to all of the Sato interests." He stepped through the door and walked away.

"You believe him?" Sofie asked. Like all the Executive liaisons to the Elite families, his loyalty was fluid.

"He didn't know about Sato's kid business. He's probably just covering his ass." Rick glanced over to the door. "I don't like all the theories floating our way. I mean, we're used to dealing with Nhu and Haadiya poking at our cases, but this time it feels like someone is trying to distract us from the real problem."

And they were all pushing them to treat the protests as the priority when Sofie was convinced they were a symptom.

14

The next morning, Sofie made some notes about the upcoming interviews while she waited for Rick to meet her. The three people involved in the sorting and distribution of meds would be on shift in an hour, and she wanted to be there before they began working.

Her mind kept going to the meds as the reason people were getting ill. She'd taken a double dose of her own because she couldn't risk even a few symptoms showing while she talked to medical professionals. It was easy to hide her condition from people like Rick or Llewelyn. But someone used to diagnosing patients? Even if they didn't immediately see the early symptoms of a Fades attack, they would notice her tremors and start asking questions.

"Ready?" Rick asked as he strolled up with a cup of stim-juice.

Sofie took it and sipped, letting the sweet and tangy Rellian blufroot flood her with energy. Or maybe that was just the stim-juice. "We'll start by asking if they noticed anything odd recently," she said.

Rick led the way toward the higher levels of Manufacturing. The food and meds were created in a clean environment far from the dirt and sweat of the machine shops and grease factories. Medical processing was the only section on the Mallet that spanned two castes. Their current destination was staffed by Support workers.

"I like it as a plan."

The corridors and streets of Support were clear of protesters still. It wouldn't stay that way, if her suspicions were correct. Sofie could almost feel the pressure of bodies around her chanting and demanding change as she walked beside Rick. The ringleaders were up to something, but it wasn't her problem right now. With luck it would never be her problem.

They entered the office where Kivi, Lu, and Gold worked. All the administration for medical services on the Mallet was conducted in one location. No receptionist waited to greet them. The building had a security system to keep out unwanted visitors. The system also provided clear directions to the current location of a person if the visitor had the right code. The police always had the right code.

"It looks like Kivi is closest," Sofie said. "We'll tag all three so if anyone leaves unexpectedly, we'll know."

She typed the names into the security system. Three data films slid out of an opening at her hand height. She handed Lu's and Gold's to Rick and then watched as a green light indicated Kivi's position and a crawling blue path leading from their location in the lobby. A name would appear on each door as they passed because wandering around in blank corridors was disorienting.

. . .

Anna Kivi was at her desk reading reports from a large screen. Blond haired and petite, she wouldn't stand out in a crowd. She looked up when Sofie knocked on the open door. "Yes?"

Knowing the person dropping by was authorized must give her a sense of safety, Sofie thought. "Police. We have a few questions." She wasn't sure why she'd put it that way instead of in a softer tone. Her words weren't exactly harsh, but the absence of a greeting and introduction made her sound curt. Her subconscious must be trying to put Anna Kivi on guard.

"Have a seat," Kivi said, pointing to two chairs across her desk. Not even remotely reacting to Sofie's brusqueness. "What can I do to help?"

"We're investigating the recent spike in illnesses," Rick said. "What do you know about the situation?"

Sofie took out her pad and started taking notes. The pad would record the interview, but writing their answers down unnerved some people. And that way Rick could lead the interview and she could observe.

"I understand it's the Maintenance workers?" Kivi said.

"Some from other castes," Rick said. "But yes, mostly Maintenance."

"It's not environmental?"

"It may be their conditions are being affected by an environmental change," Rick said. "We're here because there's a possibility the meds are the cause. Have you seen anything unusual in the last week?"

Sofie noticed Kivi's eyes flick to her screen before she answered. To give herself time to come up with a lie? Or was she distracted by work?

"The supplies are the same as always. No new manufacturing or raw material changes. It's very unlikely the cause lies here," she said.

"It's very early in the investigation and we're talking to a number of people. We'll narrow it down to a suspect soon. What makes you think something else must be the cause?" Rick gave her the grin that melted most people's resistance.

Sofie waited for Kivi's answer. If it was true, she should have no problem giving them a solid reason no one here was involved. Her whole job was to ensure the safety of the supply of medications. Not just the chronic condition meds, but treatment for everything from a scratch to a fatal sickness.

"If it was something we missed here, far more people would be affected. As it is, you have too small a sample to point to supply issues." Kivi settled back in her chair as if she'd passed a test.

"True," Rick said. "I'm sure you're right. If you say you haven't seen anything odd, I believe you. As I said, we have more people to interview. Thanks for your time." He stood and motioned for Sofie to join him.

"I hope you find the answer soon, Detective." Kivi turned back to her screen as if they weren't still in her office.

Outside, Sofie activated Selma Gold's data film. They followed that path until she was sure they were out of Anna Kivi's earshot. "Lying."

"Yeah. I think so too. But everyone lies on the Mallet. Do you think it's about our case?" Rick pulled her to the side.

"I don't have anything concrete, yet. But she said nothing's changed, and we know it has. You think she's ignorant of the problem or trying to stop us following that lead?"

"We'll find out eventually," Rick said. "I got the feeling she was covering up something, but it might just be something at work — a problem employee, maybe."

Sofie checked the hallway in case someone was approaching. "If she knows something, maybe she was misdirecting us. Maybe the change is something we didn't think to ask about. Let's get onto our next interview."

"Shit," Rick said, pointing to Selma Gold's data film. "She's heading out of the building. Should we abandon Deva Lu and follow?"

Sofie pulled up the schedule she'd requested for the three workers. "No. We should have interviewed her first. She's assigned to review the incoming shipments." How had she missed that timing issue? "We'll do Deva Lu and then go to the incoming Temporaries to talk to Gold afterwards."

When they followed Deva Lu's tracer, they found a tall man in a lecture hall with a handful of students.

"Ah, I'm sure the audience will be happy for an early dismissal," he said. "What can I do to help?"

When the lecture hall was empty, Sofie explained the purpose of their visit. He nodded slowly.

"I heard about that. I'm afraid I assumed it was some problem in Maintenance. I hear the conditions there are appalling."

"It's not only Maintenance," Sofie said.

She watched as Deva applied that to some internal knowledge base, his eyes losing focus on anything external. "You think there has been a change in the efficacy of the various treatments."

He got there fast. "It's one of the possibilities we're considering."

"Hmm. I hope not. Too many of us rely on medication to get through our days." He pinched his nose and closed his eyes. Sofie couldn't stop imagining his actions as triggers to a thought process. Like he was an organic computer. "A change in the process would be an indicator, yes?"

"We haven't had any luck finding anything odd," Rick said.

"The only thing I can pinpoint is my new position. I was transferred to the training area two weeks ago."

"Why?" Sofie asked.

"My supervisor thought we needed fresh eyes on the reconciliation. I was happy to take on the new responsibility, but I was surprised that no one has yet replaced me."

A vacant position meant a gap in oversight. "Who is your supervisor?" She thought she knew the answer.

"Anna Kivi. I never got along with her, but you don't expect your boss to be a friend after all. She could be quite harsh without much provocation. She did know her job, though, so I expect her to be very successful at whatever she does."

Another thing that had changed. Kivi knew about it and the risk involved. So why hadn't she said anything?

15

Sofie sent Rick to interview Selma Gold and then headed back to the bullpen. She needed to be behind the security firewalls to fit this new information into the soup of data they were trying to organize. It definitely felt like a pattern was emerging around the three people responsible for reconciling the inventory of meds. She'd schedule time to interview the inspectors in Manufacturing at her office when she got back.

"Detective."

The quiet voice pulled Sofie out of her tight focus on the case. She'd lost herself in her thoughts and didn't immediately recognize her surroundings. *I'm in Support. No unrest evident.* She'd been stupid to let her attention lapse. Support may be safe on a normal day, but the protesters had been infiltrating, so she couldn't rely on it remaining that way.

"Here," the voice sounded again.

This time she located the speaker. In the corridor to her right. A head peeked around the corner of the store. Tall, gender unclear, wrapped in dark, loose clothing. A scarf hid the face.

"Come out," Sofie commanded. After berating herself for wandering around in a fog, she was not going to join a disguised stranger in a side alley.

"Just come closer," the person said. The voice was deep with a roughness that made Sofie think it was a man.

She stepped to the side of the alley entrance, out of range of a grabbing hand. The walkway was deserted on this side of the square, so no witnesses if the encounter went wrong. The police station was just in sight down a side street, which gave her confidence. "Who sent you? And why?"

"Who do you think?"

The way the man was dressed and his need to stay hidden told Sofie he'd come from the dark streets. "The boss?" If he or she felt it necessary to send a messenger, something was very bad. No one knew who ran the clump of streets and squares comprising the criminal center of the Mallet, but whoever it was generally kept their business and residents inside.

"Good guess," he whispered. "You need to listen. I'm out of here as soon as I finish."

Sofie reached for her pad.

"No recording. It's not long or complicated."

"Fine, go ahead. You aren't the only one with things to do."

"The boss says you're taking too long to solve this case. That people are coming to the dark streets looking for supplies to hoard — drugs, medical and recreational, and food if they can afford it. Expecting some big trouble. The boss says you need to fix this, or we'll take action. You won't like what we'll do to protect our streets. Our business relies on a miserable but peaceful population."

Threats coming from all directions made a case almost

impossible to solve. The Elite families might be more subtle, but they were planning the same actions as the boss of the dark streets if Sofie didn't solve this fast.

"It's one station," Sofie said. "If part of it goes down, everyone goes down."

"Yeah, well, the fucking Elites aren't the only ones with escape plans."

"You think the boss will take all the people in his control with him? He'll get out with a few he trusts. He'll set up somewhere else and recruit local talent to provide services."

"Maybe I'm one of the trusted few." There was a touch of uncertainty in his voice.

"Maybe your boss is an Elite and won't take anyone." The idea that an Elite family ran the dark streets wasn't new to Sofie. Not many people had enough clout to set up and maintain the kind of business that went on there. And commerce was commerce. Credits didn't carry any moral stain when they passed through the bottom line.

"Maybe I'm the boss," the voice said.

Sofie dashed the two steps to the corner and turned into the alley, hoping to catch him before he could move. All she saw was the flick of a cloak hem as the messenger turned a corner. No point in giving chase. He'd be long gone by the time she reached the intersection. If she really thought it was the boss, she'd be racing to find him while scanning for drone cameras.

If people were expecting violence, hoarding wouldn't be the end of it. The workers would find reasons to stay close to home, so processing would stop. The outgoing product would dry up. Contract penalties would come into play. Incoming shipments would halt, and they received more than just ore to be processed. It would affect the people who bought the product from the Mallet's clients. The corporations would look elsewhere for the processes the Mallet could no longer provide.

The population would die out from starvation, sickness, and violence. At some point, the Mallet would be easy pickings for other corporations, and the Elites would be gone. In her experience, changes like that didn't make for improvements. The survivors would never get out of debt for damages. New people would carry a bigger burden on their contracts.

If solving the case would prevent all that, then Sofie wouldn't stop until she found out what was happening, and who was behind it.

16

S ofie sent a message to update Rick as soon as she closed the door of the case room behind her. The warning from the dark streets boss was just one more distraction. It didn't matter what anyone else wanted; Sofie would get to the bottom of this incident. Even if she couldn't put a stop to corruption completely, she could end this crime and the next and the next until she couldn't do the job any longer.

While she waited for Rick to call, Sofie closed her eyes and ran a check on her body. She'd been free of symptoms for a week thanks to Bindes upping her dosage. Far from making her feel confident the Fades were under control, the absence of symptoms made her worry the next attack was just waiting for her to relax. She thought about her finger-tips and how her symptoms always started there. No tingling, no coldness, no tremors. She felt her shoulders drop with relief. Her body felt healthy, but a mean little voice said she could just be fooling herself. Once that voice started talking, there was no point in trying to argue with it. Ignoring it sometimes made it go away.

Sofie opened her eyes and started sorting through the notes from the interviews, preparing to call a formal interview for Anna Kivi. Because she was from Support, they would need to justify the inconvenience. Approval from Llewelyn was enough, and he usually wasn't too picky about the strength of the rationale.

Petra's face appeared in a square in the bottom corner of her pad. Sofie tapped to accept and exchanged greetings.

"I'm glad I caught you," Petra said. "Good news."

Sofie smiled encouragement but knew that one person's good news could be another's bad.

"The patients are recovering." Petra's smile got wider. "All at different paces, but definitely improving."

"Wonderful." Something to ease the pressure coming from the protesters, at least. "Are they well enough to be interviewed?"

Petra's smile dimmed. "Not yet. Can I call you when I think it's safe? I don't want anyone worried. Fear can have a negative impact on recovery."

People suddenly recovering didn't undo the original crime. There were other interviews to conduct, and it wasn't a guarantee that the patients would have anything useful to share. Unless their meds looked different, they probably had no idea what went wrong. "Yes. Did anything unusual happen? Any visitors? A new nurse or doctor?"

"I didn't think to investigate. Let me check." The call screen showed Petra's face as she put Sofie on hold.

If the perpetrator knew the police were getting close, maybe they stopped? No guarantee it was anything to do with Kivi, Lu, or Gold. Everything that happened in their building might be under surveillance. Someone else getting nervous because those three were under scrutiny?

The image of Petra's face flickered and then the woman

was back on the call. "I checked and no one visited. We'd have a record, or they'd be on camera at some point. No new hires or temp staff. The only difference was the medication. We received a new batch this morning."

A warmth flooded Sofie's body at the knowledge they were right. "Were you expecting a delivery?"

Petra checked something off-screen and then turned back. "It's the regular timing, but we got some Maintenance-branded doses. It could be because of the number of Maintenance patients, but that would defeat the purpose of the branding. Hang on again. I'll check with the reception clerk. He signed for it."

Before Sofie could say she'd come to interview him, Petra hit the hold button again.

"Hey," Rick said as he stepped into the room. "I caught the Gold woman on the way back to the office. She hasn't noticed anything odd. Here." He handed her a large stim-juice and a greasy pastry. "She said she'd call us if anything came up. And she doesn't like her boss, either."

Sofie sipped the stim-juice. Perfectly flavored. "Let me guess. Anna Kivi?"

"Says she's a micro-managing bitch." He glanced over her shoulder at Sofie's pad but didn't comment on the call.

Sofie gave him an update. "We still need to check this discrepancy through the process, I guess."

"I'll find out who signed off on the shipment for delivery," Rick said.

"I'm back," Petra said. "He did call the distributor. He thought it was an error, but no. They're sending extra supplies in case any area is cut off by the protests."

A good reason, but also a reasonable excuse if it was to draw attention from the effects of the original crime.

"Thanks," Sofie said. "We'll need to interview your

reception clerk when we come in for the patients." They ended the call and Sofie added the new interviews to the action list on the wall.

"We should split up," Rick said. "This afternoon. I can talk to the reception guy. I can take the distribution research. Leaves you available for when the patients can talk."

"And I can get the paperwork done while you're out solving the case," Sofie said.

"Never occurred to me," Rick said, batting his eyes in innocence. "What do you want to do about the warning from the dark streets?"

"Is there anything to do about it?" The warning hadn't come with any personal threats. And it was just another voice chattering the same words.

The door opened. Amanda held it open after she took a step inside. "Llewelyn wants to talk to you about your progress."

Sofie motioned for Rick to keep working and followed Amanda.

17

"I received a report that the crisis is over," Llewelyn said without preamble. "How long will it take to wrap everything up? We'll be giving the news to the media in a couple of hours."

"I can't wrap this up," Sofie said. She struggled to find a way to ask who told him without getting reprimanded. Llewelyn was usually informal, but someone had him tied up in knots about this case, which made him unpredictable. "If we don't find out the cause, it will happen again. The next time will be worse, you know that. Can I ask who told you we were finished?"

Amanda took a step closer to Sofie. Maybe a warning to stop talking. Unlikely to be a gesture of support.

"The situation with the unrest is getting worse," Llewelyn said. "We need everyone ready to act if it escalates to actual violence. Our sources tell us that is very possible."

So he doesn't want me to know who's going behind my back. "If they find out we've shut down this case without a solution, won't that make it worse?" Sofie asked. "I thought the reason things got this bad was because we didn't care about sick Maintenance and Manufacturing workers."

Llewelyn flipped open a file and glanced at the contents, then looked back at Sofie. "Not everyone agrees that's the cause. I can't let you run with this case forever. How long do you need? What resources do I need hold back from peace-keeping?"

Sofie thought through the list of interviews and unanswered questions on the wall. Normally they would be working to add names to a pool of suspects at this point, then narrow down to one or two. Her gut told her that Anna Kivi was at least involved, if not the perpetrator. But they had no motive beyond some kind of greed. And that was too common a motive to be of any use calming the protesters. There was also a danger that the investigation would start looking only for proof that Kivi was the suspect and miss the real criminal if she was innocent.

But if riots broke out while they were still investigating, it wouldn't help to assign blame to someone. At the point of violence, no one would be listening.

"It's only been a day," she said. "Give me until tonight to answer you. You know we aren't dragging things out. We never do."

Llewelyn pursed his lips and stared at her for a long moment. Sofie knew better than to speak at this point. He needed time to process, and interrupting him would not give her the answer she needed.

"Until tonight," he said. "I can spare you some help for this morning, but after that I need results. And I expect something concrete, Allen. Otherwise, we're closing the case. I need people on the streets."

Sofie stood and thanked him. "If I can have Amanda's

help for an hour? We have a ton of data and she's good at seeing patterns."

18

I n the case room, Sofie projected the process flow of meds approval and reconciliation on the wall for Amanda to study.

"Is this where you think the problem starts?" Amanda asked. "Someone manipulating the distribution? What about in Manufacturing?"

Sofie explained they'd found little in the way of discrepancies in their data, but the interviews seemed to point to Anna Kivi being the only one who had enough power to do anything fishy.

"And for some reason she lied to us. We thought about the manufacturing processes, but the medications for the affected conditions aren't only made on the Mallet," Sofie said.

"I'm off to talk to the inspectors," Rick said. "Unless you want me to hang around?"

Sofie told him to head out. She had Amanda for an hour and couldn't afford to waste any of it chatting. "I'll send you anything we find. It might give you more questions, right?"

When Rick left, Sofie turned back to Amanda. The woman had not taken her focus off the projection.

"There are a few spots where the process loops back," she said. "Each time it's to your suspect."

Suspect was a strong word for Anna Kivi, but Sofie chose not to correct Amanda. "Is there a good reason for the loop?" All processes on the Mallet were as efficient as possible to save credits.

Amanda didn't answer. She walked alongside the projection, reading off the steps in the process, touching the wall periodically and mumbling. When she finished the first pass, she turned away from it. "Okay, there are only a few reasons to loop a process like this. First, there's a point where errors can be introduced normally, no criminal intent, but enough to warrant a second look. And a good place to make adjustments if you're skimming. It's not really a loop, but a separate process tied into the original."

If that was the reason, Sofie understood the need for diligence. Meds were too important for cavalier oversight. But inventory control? How would an error in numbers be that big a problem?

"Yeah," Amanda said, reading Sofie's expression. "Not likely. The error here would be in numbers. A little leeway is fine, and who's going to innocently miscount enough doses to make it profitable?"

"Are they just checking units?" Sofie wasn't ready to let go of her only viable lead.

"No, batches and intake and expiry data, too." Amanda glanced behind her to check the wall again. "It would have to be a pretty elaborate scheme to be here. If someone is messing with the batches — that's what you think, right?"

Sofie nodded, not willing to tell Amanda anything that might taint her fresh look.

"They'd need to move the actual product around. That's going to be noticed. You can't just stick a bunch of pills in your purse and walk away. For this to be worthwhile, it would involve taking cases, or a big percentage of every case."

"And the other reason to loop a process?" Sofie didn't want to focus on what was looking like a bad idea.

"Someone got caught stealing. So whoever regulates it puts in another checkpoint, and no one bothers to confirm if it's needed."

Sofie leaned forward. "I don't remember anyone getting charged with something like that."

"It would be covered up. It's Support, right? The person was probably demoted and that's it."

"Can we tell how long ago?" Sofie's instincts were creating flutters in her gut.

Amanda expanded the view on the process. "You'll need to request older versions. You think someone took advantage of the change? It's a long shot, but not impossible."

"If this started out small a few years ago, it would be easy to expand whatever they were doing by tiny increments, right?"

"Let me get my pad," Amanda said. She hustled out of the room.

While she waited, Sofie tried to estimate the volume someone would need to make stealing worthwhile. Amanda was right: unless the price was astronomical on a black market somewhere, only large volumes made sense. It had to be happening at a shipping point.

"I've requested the last four versions of the process," Amanda said as she entered the room. "What exactly do you think might be happening?"

"It's not quite an organized theory," Sofie said. "I think

it's to do with expiring meds. Someone is extending the life on the label, but the potency is gone. That's why people are getting sick. But like you said, it's not possible that someone is taking crates of product. If they are selling off the new shipments, it has to be happening somewhere other than in an office." So much for Anna Kivi being a suspect.

"I've got the older versions of the process," Amanda said. "It pays to be the boss's assistant; you get all kinds of line-jumping authority."

Sofie watched the image on the wall flick out as older steps were added. "How far back?"

"These? Six years. Pretty standard changes. But the one we want is here." She pointed to a projected step on the wall. "Two years ago. So, long enough for your theory that it started out small."

If the scheme started that long ago and no one noticed, what had changed?

"What do you think is happening?" Sofie asked.

"I'd need to do a lot more analysis to get good answers, and I've given you the hour you asked for. There are a few places where it could work. If the incoming shipments were not what they say on the label, then we're not getting the meds we need from off-station. But you say it's not just one source that's causing illness. And there still needs to be collaborators on the Mallet to make it work." She sighed and walked along the wall again.

Sofie waited. This was Amanda's strength. When she was in analyst mode, she wasn't annoying and didn't seem to need to snipe and criticize. Sofie admitted this was a skill she didn't possess beyond a minimal competence. Alone, she found data confusing, but Amanda didn't need to bounce ideas off anyone to see the clues.

"Okay. Whoever is doing this has had time to build a

network or to work out a way to be a lone operator. If it's a network, you'll find someone, probably in shipping or distribution, who'll fold. If it's a lone operator, you need to find the person most able to hide the skimming. And soon. Something made them escalate, and now the sickness is a problem for them because it's attracted our interest."

Amanda checked the time and pressed her lips together. Sofie saw the frustration in her frown and the flick of her gaze to the wall again. "Sorry. I have to go."

Before Sofie could think of a way to keep Amanda engaged, she strode out and crossed the bullpen to enter Llewelyn's office.

19

Too many suspects. Sofie stared at the wall. If this plan was long-term, what could have pushed the perpetrator to escalate now? Like Amanda said, something had done just that, and the result was a police investigation. Whoever they were looking for was cashing out. And maybe the protests were ignited to take resources away from an investigation long enough for the culprit to escape. Amanda's time hadn't been wasted, even though she failed to reveal a clue. Now Sofie and Rick had a direction within the data. Maybe the answer was on the wall right now.

She sorted the medication list into two groups: what came from off-station, and what they manufactured on the Mallet. Nothing popped out as a lead, other than to confirm the plan likely wasn't confined to shipping. To mess with both types of medication meant interference somewhere near or within the distribution process.

Rick messaged her. *On my way back. Have you eaten?*

She answered and gave him her food order. Maybe

eating would give her new insights. While she waited, Sofie created a list of roles involved for the two tracks: meds shipped in and meds manufactured. Boring work, but she hoped to see where in the whole list of jobs someone could steal enough to make it worth risking death.

She was still staring at the wall of job titles when Rick came in with a bag full of unhealthy but delicious food that smelled of fried dough and sugar, but contained plain roast vegetable sandwiches. Rick must have eaten donuts on his way back.

"The inspectors look clean," Rick said as he laid out the food on the table. "They haven't had any concerns about quality. They sample each batch to test it, and if there's even a half-percent variance, it gets rejected. No excess rejections lately. What's this?" He pointed to the new information on the wall.

Sofie updated him on Amanda's findings while she ate, hoping recounting the story would add some inspiration. "So we have big-time pressure on the case and it's not getting more focused."

"Not true," Rick said. "If we all think it's being done here on the Mallet, then we've defined the scope."

Sofie sat up. "Where else could it be happening?"

He ate the last of his sandwich and tossed the packaging in the bin. "There are only a few raw materials on the Mallet. Yeah, we grow some food, but most of the components for the fertilizer and soil are imported. That's true about most things."

"So this could be from off-station? I'd discounted that, but maybe the people here are just following orders?"

They wouldn't be able to solve a crime that didn't originate on the Mallet. And they probably couldn't prove anyone on the Mallet was complicit. Sofie's gut told her that only a culprit from the Mallet would satisfy the protesters. Sometimes the truth just wasn't enough.

"You think someone off-station isn't involved?" Rick woke his pad. "My guess is we'll find someone here, but the reason for the skimming and the pressure to accelerate the plan are coming from off-station. Where do you want to start?"

"Money," Sofie said. "Now that we have an idea of what's going on, we get the names of anyone who could be a suspect and look for a pile of credits."

Excess credit wouldn't mean they had their perpetrator; too many people on the Mallet were involved in embezzling, skimming, or black-marketeering. But it would narrow the field of suspects.

Rick grabbed his stim-juice, continuing to type record requests with one hand. "I've requested a list of everyone in the key positions we know about. What about the people we've eliminated already?"

"Key positions?" Sofie asked.

"Yeah, from the process flows. I have a friend in records; he'll do the initial draw for the jobs."

"How did you define key positions?"

"Anyone with authority to approve or reconcile any inventory, production, or distribution. From the front bay to the back. We'll get hundreds, probably."

Three more names wouldn't matter if they turned out to be leads. "Add Gold, Kivi, and Lu if they don't come up as key jobs. I'm not sure we can rely on what we've already decided about them."

When Rick finished the query and they were waiting for results, Sofie asked, "How do you know you can trust this friend?" What if they'd chosen the wrong process? Records would be an easy place to manipulate anything. A good hacker could hide any evidence of changes to data records. No point in pursuing a trail that wouldn't give them a chance of closing the case.

"We participated in a rather wild sexual event recently. He and I have no secrets," Rick said with a smirk. "Well, I have secrets obviously, but him? No."

Rick's wide range of sexual partners and experiences came in handy once in a while. Sofie didn't remember him being a good enough lover to make her bend the rules.

Maybe his imagination could stretch to more than sex. "How would you do it? Steal meds, I mean."

Rick pushed his pad to the side and leaned back to stare at the ceiling as if reading his plan.

"I'd make sure no one noticed. I'd have off-station contacts who could move the legit product, and I'd have a credit account somewhere with big privacy laws. I'd bypass the whole manufacturing and approval process, let them run clean. I'd do the switch before the meds were distributed."

They could start the search there. "Good idea, but that's a pretty tightly controlled system."

"The individual couriers?" Rick suggested. "Remember, I'd keep it small. I'm sure the couriers get bribed for everything, so they wouldn't suspect anything unusual was happening."

"But who needs our meds?" That was Sofie's sticking point. Why? Any planet or space station who needed medications could get them. Nothing cost so much that it would be worth stealing.

"It would have to be criminal, right?" Rick said, straightening up. "Some unauthorized colony, some major criminal organization that can't just put in an order for what they need."

"And if it's not just about money?" Weakening the Mallet could create all kinds of opportunities.

"Then we're screwed."

20

S ofie stretched and then stood. "You know what? We aren't going to find the answer in these lists. Let's go check out what happens in the incoming Temporaries. Maybe we're relying on what should happen when something completely different is actually going on."

Rick laughed. "You mean someone not following procedure? How original." He packed his pad and checked his weapon. "It's the best idea you've had, you know."

Sofie tucked her pad in an inside pocket of her jacket. "You think we're going to run into problems?" She nodded at his stun gun.

"You should read the department notices. All personnel to be prepared for situations requiring containment."

She checked the charge on her own stunner. "I hope we don't need these up front. That would mean a hell of an escalation."

Their path to the incoming Temporaries section took Sofie and Rick farther away from the problem areas. If they ran into protests in Support again, or in Authority, it would mean the unrest was already out of control, even if the protesters were non-violent.

Outside the bullpen, Sofie noted a crowd in the corner of the square. Some people were holding up holo signs. *Stop the poisoning* and *make the Elite's pay*. The last would get them a fine — at the very least — if any of the nine families decided to cause problems about the idea of compensation, or a misplaced apostrophe. She hoped the Prathams had enough sense to know responding to the signs would spark the violence everyone was working to avoid.

"Poisoning?" Sofie was starting to feel out of the loop. The protests weren't her case, but it did look like they were fueled by it. "Didn't the announcement about recoveries go out?"

"Not yet, but it won't help. Someone is pushing an agenda here. Feeding these idiots what they want to hear so they can feel justified in acting out." Rick checked his pad. "Oh, I was wrong, the update was broadcast a few minutes ago."

"Let's get out of here before we're sidelined to deal with this," Sofie said as three riot-gear-clad officers marched toward the crowd.

The holo signs blinked off and the crowd dispersed before the police got close enough to act.

"I guess they aren't committed enough to spend a few hours in jail," Rick said.

Sofie wasn't sure he'd read the action correctly. If these protests ended at the sight of authority, she figured it was only to pop up somewhere else. "Let's hope that's it," she said.

. . .

THEY ARRIVED in the Temporaries section without encountering more disgruntled mobs. The peace hadn't stopped Sofie from scanning everyone they passed for a protest badge. She caught Rick doing the same. "You'd think everything was normal if you lived here," she said.

He nodded without turning away from his inspection of their surroundings. "I guess that's part of their point."

A tall woman with her hair shaved close to her scalp approached. She was dressed in the gray overalls that seemed to be a uniform for the few people passing through the corridor behind her. Something had changed since the last time Sofie ranged this far.

"Your business?" the woman asked, her voice rasping.

"We're on a case," Sofie said. "Just here to observe for background information." Something was telling Sofie to keep everything on a cold, professional level.

"Your identification?"

Sofie and Rick showed their pads with the ID displayed.

"You have any authorization?"

"Like I said. We're observing," Sofie said. Technically, cops didn't work either Temporaries, but until lately the requirement for documentation had been ignored. Torque only stopped troublemakers from joining in the permanent parties in the outgoing Temporaries. Only the actual bays were off-limits. This end of the Mallet wasn't known for its parties, but it also wasn't usually so tightly controlled.

The woman stood her ground. "What do you expect to find?"

Rick touched Sofie's elbow, a signal to let him take over. Maybe his charm would get them through.

"Nothing," Rick said with a smile. "I'm sure you have the whole area running smoothly. But we're hoping to put a few boundaries around a crime. To make sure it's all Mallet, no off-station interests."

He'd taken a step toward the woman, not threatening, but including her as part of their team. Sofie had no idea how he projected the difference, but even she was seeing them as three allies.

"Your crime?" Her voice was softer than before.

"I'm sure you understand we need to keep the details confidential," Rick said, smiling even broader.

"You have an hour." She stepped aside. "Turn left at the end of the passageway and someone will be there to escort you."

Sofie paused as she passed the woman. "Can I ask what's changed? It's quite different here."

"I work for a private security organization. We run the incoming now."

That changed the dynamic between the cops and the Temporaries. Before, there was a council of sorts in both Temporaries that worked with the station authorities. A professional security team was too much like a second police force. How would the usual skimming and other corruption work on the Mallet if no one could be bribed to let unofficial imports in?

"How long have you been here? Oh, and welcome to the Mallet." Sofie tried to soften the interrogation.

"Three days," the woman answered. She looked at her pad. "You have fifty-seven minutes."

Their escort asked what they wanted to observe and then led them to a bay and stood to the side. Now that they were in the working part of the incoming bays, Sofie could see the workers were dressed as usual. Generally in overalls, but in different colors. Those wearing gray ones were grouped close to the entrances. Fifty or so private security guards in this bay alone. She glanced at Rick, but he was observing the workers. She pulled out her pad to send Llewelyn a heads-up about the professionals in case no one had informed him.

"No recordings," the guard said.

For a moment she considered explaining but decided it could wait until they were away from the section.

"You done?" the guard asked.

"The crates are coming through those doors," Rick said. "What's on the other side?"

"The cargo doors of the transports. We stay on this side."

No evidence of any deviation in the processes. No crates were dropped, no workers stepping out of the flow of traffic. However this manipulation of the meds was being done, it was all Mallet.

21

"So what now?" Rick asked as soon as they stepped away from the guarded entrance to the Temporaries.

"I guess eliminating the incoming supplies as a source of meddling is a good thing. Just not a step forward." Sofie tried to think of some other place to search for this particular form of corruption but kept coming back to the reconciling steps. It was the only place that dealt with both off-station and on-station inventory. "If the money is being made by smuggling meds to another station or a planet, Torque might know."

"When were you last in the outgoing Temporaries?" Rick asked as he started walking. "Maybe the security there has been outsourced too."

Unlikely, Sofie thought. If something so drastic happened, Torque would have gotten the message to her — unless he couldn't. She pulled out her pad to search for any news of a change in the outgoing Temporaries. Nothing in the last few weeks popped up. It didn't reassure her because something had changed in the front and not been reported.

"We should head there," she said. "I can't believe it happened without us knowing. I mean, this end of the Mallet leads to Authority and is kind of buffered. Outgoing is right next door, so to speak. We'd hear from someone if the parties were shut down."

"True," Rick said. "Maybe you should drop in on Torque soon. Just in case."

"So I guess we go back to Kivi, Gold, and Lu?" Sofie said. She didn't like the idea since she'd already mentally eliminated the three from their suspect list, but logically someone in that building had to know something. "Actually, maybe we should talk to different people there. We might have been wrong about the level of authority needed to conduct the scam."

Rick dug in his pocket but came up empty. "Do you have the tracers?"

The initial tracers had led them to their three targets. "No. I'm not sure they would work at this range anyway. And didn't they have an expiry?"

"Okay, I thought it would be good to know where Gold, Kivi, and Lu were if we intend to interview people who report to them."

"We can get new tracers when we go in." Sofie wondered if the directory would show them the hierarchy, so they didn't need to get tracers on everyone working there. "Maybe Amanda can pull some names for us."

Her pad chimed with an incoming message before she could contact Amanda. Petra Starlight. *Please come to the ward. I have news.*

She showed the message to Rick. "We'll go there first," she said. "The interviews can wait until we can get organized."

It took long enough to get to the clinic that Sofie was

able to send the information request to Amanda and receive a list of names while they were on the way.

When they walked through the lobby of the clinic, the reception counter was empty. Petra rushed out to meet them, pressing her lips together and shaking her head when Sofie asked for the news. Pointing in the direction of her office area, Petra led them back, flicking on her privacy screen as soon as they were stuffed into the small space.

"We've had three deaths," she said. "Two patients passed in the night. It wasn't a real surprise. They were declining despite our efforts. Underlying conditions, you understand."

Sofie didn't, but she let the statement stand. Petra wouldn't have called them in to share that news. "The other death?"

Petra nodded and pulled a thin file from the stack on her desk. "Yes. This person was rushed in two hours ago. No chronic illness, so they weren't taking any of the meds we're watching. And they worked in the medical supply chain."

So not just another Maintenance worker.

"You think this is related?" Rick asked. "I mean, people die all the time, right?"

Petra flipped the file open and glanced at the top print-out. "Yes. People in the physical jobs. Maintenance and Manufacturing are dangerous places to work. Accidents are common. But for a teacher to die, suddenly? That's rare."

An ice ball formed in Sofie's gut, and she felt Rick tense beside her. "Name?"

"Deva Lu."

"Cause of death?" Sofie figured it was result of being questioned by the police, but that wouldn't be the official cause.

"Right now, unknown, but I've ordered an autopsy." Petra closed the file and pushed it toward Sofie. "Your copy."

Deva Lu had been healthy enough when she talked to him earlier. "What's your best guess?"

"The only thing I can think is that it means the man was purposely killed. Poison or some injury that we didn't notice. If someone damaged a vital organ with a laser, it could take a day or two to kill."

"You'll let us know the results of the autopsy?" Sofie asked.

"I've asked for an expedited examination," Petra said. "I also asked them to screen for a list of poisons that fit the progression and symptoms."

"And if anyone else dies," Rick said, "we need to know as soon as it happens."

"I'll do my best. But if this situation has spread beyond these patients, I'm not the only doctor here, and we're not the only clinic in the section."

Sofie thanked her, put the file under her arm, and led Rick out of the clinic. "You think the protesters knew someone was going to die that way?" she asked as they headed back to the bullpen.

"You think they poisoned someone to make a point?" Rick asked. "I doubt it, but maybe the killer let something leak to escalate the protests."

"Or it was an extremely good guess." It was more urgent than ever to go back and interview Deva Lu's co-workers. "We need to talk to his students, or new boss, or anyone who might have known him."

"Later," Rick said, holding up his pad. "We've been called back to the office."

Sofie checked. Yes, the alert was flashing, and that could be nothing but bad news.

22

W hen Sofie and Rick arrived at the bullpen, it was filling up with cops, including some Sofie knew were not on duty. The streets in Support were quiet, and no one loitered outside in the square, but Maintenance was very different from Support.

Sofie noticed Amanda leave Llewelyn's side and angle through the bullpen to intercept them on their way to the case room.

"Rick, report to Shehata, he's heading the crowd control group," Amanda said.

He paused for a beat and then handed Sofie his pad. "You'll need my notes. I'll send you a guest access code."

"And me?" Sofie asked. If the situation with the protests had escalated enough, no other case would take priority.

"Dump your stuff and report to Llewelyn," Amanda said. "Did you get anywhere?"

For the first time Sofie believed Amanda was simply interested and had no agenda. "We've got a death now. And maybe a lead."

Amanda was looking out over the cops who were

forming groups of three or four, waiting for Sargent Shehata to give orders. "That's good news."

"And there's private security in the incoming Temporaries. Know anything about it?" If there was something going on, Amanda would be able find out, if she didn't already know.

"Llewelyn has more details on that. Report ASAP."

Sofie took two minutes to lock up the pads and documents in the case room. If they were going to be reassigned, their notes and records would be better off secured. She considered taking a med, but with no symptoms, decided the risk of overdoing the treatment was too high. If an attack started in the middle of the action, she wanted to have meds on hand.

"Come," Llewelyn said, gesturing Sofie into his office. He hit the security screens and Sofie's ears popped. "Maintenance is getting to be a problem. We've kept the protests confined, but it's not going to stay that way. They're growing. I need Rick on the front lines."

"The case?" Sofie waited to be told she was to close it down for now, marshaling her argument against it. If any more unexplainable deaths happened, taking official eyes off the crime would be like giving permission to the perpetrator to keep going.

"For now, work it alone. Will that be a problem?"

"It'll slow me down."

"Don't let it drag out. If we can't get these protests to settle, I'm going to put everyone on the crowd control assignment. We're trying a show of force, so our biggest, meanest looking officers are going in."

That strategy wouldn't leave a lot of officers working ongoing investigations. "Crowd control?"

He huffed a laugh and nodded. "The powers that be

think it's less confrontational. You and I both know it's riot prevention. If you need any help on your case, I'll see what I can do, but no guarantees. A win would help a lot, Sofie. The protesters are using the sickness as kindling."

"Not just sickness now, but one death too. The protesters may have known about it before us," she said. "But I can work it alone. Has anyone suggested bringing in the private security team from up front?"

"No. They are there for the Elites. Even if they were available, it's a last resort. Mercenaries aren't good at quelling without killing. We need those people working when they stop chanting, or it's over anyway."

And we'll all be abandoned if the Mallet stops showing profit. "I'll need to go into Maintenance. What's the situation?"

Llewelyn squeezed the bridge of his nose and sighed. "It's bad; can you avoid it?"

"Probably not." If the perpetrator ran, it would be to the outgoing Temporaries. And she needed Torque's help to stop an escape. Plus, Bindes was at the Open Pit. No matter what happened with the case, she needed to get to him.

"Go as incognito as you can. Let someone know when you enter and leave. I'll update Shehata with your details. Try not to get caught up."

23

Amanda was waiting for Sofie at the door to the case room.

"I don't have time," Sofie said.

"If you need help, call me," Amanda said. "We'll be the last people they put in riot gear."

It was probably true. When it came down to putting short and thin people in riot gear, the fight might already be lost. "Thanks."

In the room, Sofie opened Rick's pad, transferred his notes, and sent him a message that she was finished with it. He could pick the device up, or not.

Staring at a wall of information felt less useful than usual. But it was vital that she didn't waste time wandering. It was late, but she might be able to track down some of Deva Lu's colleagues. She looked at the employee list and made note of the four people he seemed to be linked to for the job. She put up the hierarchy for the entire medication process. Lu's name was already struck out. No new name yet. She traced the connections between him and Anna Kivi — two more names. Then between Lu and Gold — no more names. If Lu was the intended target, then his death might not be connected to the bigger case. She added a request for his next of kin and known associates.

This was the first time she'd looked at the overall structure of the medication process instead of focusing on one or two aspects. Was there some point where supplies could be manipulated? Of course the answer was yes. Starting at the top — the Elite families. Pressure across the whole process would make it easy. A little here and a little there added up. She'd never get an Elite charged, but she could solve the case without doing so. If it was a conspiracy, someone down the line would crack and end up taking the blame.

Sofie requested the names of the incumbents in leadership positions. Time to start winnowing the list down to potential suspects. She sent a message to Shehata notifying him that she was going into Maintenance. Bindes would help her if he had anything to share, or maybe point her in a direction.

24

The trip to the Open Pit usually took ten or fifteen minutes. Today, slipping through crowds of orange-badged people without being dragged into the budding protest or being pointed out as a cop made the trip more than twice as long. The riot-gear-clad cops were doing a good job of keeping a lid on the emotions of the crowd just by being present. Rick gave her a nod as she entered the square.

Her pad pinged but Sofie didn't dare pull it out until she was safely inside the bar. The message from Rick read *Be safe.*

The only thing off about the Open Pit was the door. With it half rolled down, if things outside kicked off, the bar would be secure in seconds. Bindes was at his usual table. The regulars were not. Twenty people sat around the bar. Tables were moved into groups of four and there were boxes lined up on the bar.

"We're geared up to deal with injuries," Bindes said. "If not today, it's coming soon. So when it gets crowded outside, we get ready."

Sofie couldn't imagine how it would work. Bindes was only one man. If the boxes were full of medical supplies, they still needed skilled hands to use them. And the door would be down. But that wasn't her problem. It did make her worry that Bindes and his team had a better contact than the cops, and that riots were closer than everyone thought.

"Can you talk?"

"For now."

She looked around the bar again. The occupants were watching. "Who are they?"

"Medics and a couple of nurses I know." He looked her over intently enough for Sofie to feel uncomfortable.

"I'm fine. It's about the case. Can we go into your office?"

"That would bring more attention than you want. These people are the opposite of the usual drinkers. They're looking for some signal they can help, not actively ignoring everything around them."

And going into his office would bring that attention on her. "Fine. I need your insight on some people." She showed him the list of names she'd gleaned and explained how she'd identified them as potential suspects or victims.

"You expect me to know everyone involved?" He scanned the names and chuckled. "Okay, I do know most of these people."

A shout from outside pulled everyone's attention to the square. Nothing followed the noise, so they were still safe.

"Are any of these people likely to be stealing from the med supplies? Or poisoning someone?" The obvious answer was yes. They were on the Mallet, after all.

He ran his finger down the list and then stared at the screen, tapping his chin in thought.

Sofie found it harder than usual to sit and let Bindes

process his thoughts. Sitting in the bar with strangers while the tension from outside oozed in made her jumpier than normal. She inventoried her body for symptoms. Every time she talked about stealing or manipulating the med supply, a voice in the back of her head started yelling about an attack. Most of the time she could ignore it. But not today. So she checked her fingers; no tingling. Heart rate normal, and her thoughts seemed clear. Safe for now.

"You've looked at the hierarchy as a power structure, right?"

She nodded.

"So yes, any of these names could be your criminal, but I don't know if anyone could work in the volumes necessary to make the risk worthwhile."

"We're having trouble figuring that out too. And the poisoning?"

"Are you sure this guy was poisoned?"

She wouldn't be completely sure until she got the autopsy report. "Ninety percent, based on my experience and gut. And the doctor thinks it's a possibility."

"If you are right, anyone could be the killer. This Deva Lu could have enemies and his death could be unrelated to the meds issue."

Everything right now seemed related. The protesters were angry about people falling ill, and they'd known about the poisoning before anyone. Even Rick being pulled off the case right after they visited the incoming Temporaries and met the private security team seemed meaningful. "Until I have a concrete lead, I can't dismiss any connection."

"I can't point to one name and say they are likely to be your culprit. I also can't remove anyone from the list."

Sofie reached for her pad. She'd spent too much time

here already if he couldn't help. But Bindes didn't let go. "What?"

"The hierarchy isn't the real power structure," Bindes said. "Reporting lines blur in real life. This assumes that the people in authority are capable, but that's not always true. It is pretty easy to hide activities from a supervisor who doesn't know what you do."

That was helpful. It shouldn't be hard to find political appointees. Or lazy supervisors. "You mean I should look down the org chart, not just up it, right?"

"At the very least. If your culprit is using personal leverage, they might not even be on the list."

"Well, I can't investigate everyone on the Mallet, so I'll start with what I have." Another shout came from outside, and the screens over the bar flicked on to show the crowd. Still no active violence, but the fuse was short. "Thanks for being a sounding board."

"You're working this alone?"

She told him about Rick's reassignment. "I usually bounce ideas off him, but I know how to work alone."

"You have enough meds to get through?"

"As long as the operation is still on," she said.

"I'll let you know if anything changes. I can't see this lasting for long." He lifted his chin to point to the crowd. "It'll die down soon, or we'll be beyond worrying about the meds."

"They seem determined." Sofie looked at the screen, hoping to see a path through the crowd. "I should go before I'm stuck." She stood, thinking she might need an escort through the mess if she waited longer.

Bindes reached and took hold of her arm. "Give me another minute. I have some information on the meds."

25

ofie glanced again at the screen. The square, more crowded than before, was still peaceful. It couldn't last long. If there were other clusters of protesters in squares throughout Maintenance, jobs would be suffering. Someone would give the order to disperse the workers. Someone safe behind a desk who didn't have to face the anger of the crowd.

"Okay, but quick. I don't want to spend time in here waiting for safe passage."

"I can send you out the back. With an escort if you need it. But if you think it's more important to get back to your office, then say so."

Was she willing to put her own safety aside and hope the quality of the meds would return to normal after the case was solved? This morning, she would have said it was all the same case, that whoever was manipulating the meds was the criminal. They'd based their investigation on that assumption. Now, with poisoning on the table as a cause of the illness, their theory could be wrong. Until the autopsy results came in and the poison was identified, the whole case was a big question mark.

"It's still our best lead," she said. "Until we know other-wise, the reason those people are in the clinic is the failure of their usual treatment."

Bindes signaled one of the waiting medics, a large man with a menacing look. Someone Sofie expected to see as a bodyguard, not a medical professional. The man moved closer to the hallway leading to Bindes's office and, she suspected, the back door she didn't know existed.

"I've checked through my contacts, quietly," Bindes said. "I get my meds the same way I always have. I trust the people I deal with directly, but I can't say the same for whoever facilitates the delivery."

"How do you get them?" Sofie asked.

Bindes's expression closed. He was going to refuse to answer, too used to keeping secrets.

"If you can't tell me, I need to go."

He blinked and then gave one nod. "You're right. It's just hard to go from protecting people with silence to risking everything."

Sofie sympathized, but she had no time to help him through the hard part. "I don't need your supplier names."

"I have a few friends who overprescribe to patients. The patient leaves the extra medication at a drop point. I have no idea what compensation the patient gets."

Money, or power, or just the ability to keep living a lie. "Right now, I don't care. How does this help me?"

"There have been changes behind the scenes, and I have some names of people who've been asking questions or have taken over a job and kept up the skimming."

"Probably not at the volume they need," Sofie said. "But a lead's a lead."

"You can't leave a trail to me, or my suppliers," Bindes said as he pulled a data film out of a pocket.

"I'll do my best, but if I don't know your suppliers…"

"Nice try. Just protect me; that will take care of the rest." He handed her the data film.

Sofie placed it on her pad and read the five names. "Deva Lu is the dead man."

"Someone will take his place," Bindes said.

But there had been no hint he was involved in anything when they interviewed him. Was she losing her instincts? No, Rick hadn't seen anything either.

"Two of these are already on the list," she said. "Gold and Kivi. And the others?"

"Inspectors at the incoming Temporaries. If they are involved, it's not at the top. There are too many complex steps in this plan to ever be sure what's going on. Someone high up is directing this scheme. It's the only thing that makes sense."

Sofie added the names to her notes and returned the data film to Bindes. "It will probably help."

The bodyguard medic shifted his weight. Sofie looked at the screens. The crowd was moving toward the cops. She heard the chanting now. Time to go.

"Will this be a problem for my operation?" She wasn't sure what she wanted Bindes to say beyond what he'd said earlier.

"If this is still going on by then, your condition is the least of our worries." He nodded to the man waiting to take Sofie out of the bar. "Nothing has changed yet. Like I said, I'll send the details as soon as I have them."

Sofie followed her guide through dim hallways that branched every few feet. This was definitely not on the original plans. But so many modifications happened to facilitate life on the Mallet, it wasn't a surprise.

The man opened the door and told her to keep turning right at every intersection and she'd be close to the bullpen in five minutes.

26

S ofie made it back to the bullpen without incident. She put the new names into the case file and checked to see if she'd missed them on the various processes and charts. No. Meaning they didn't hold any official authority.

She sent a message to Rick that she was safe, apologizing for forgetting to do it when she left the bar.

No problem. Crowd dispersed. Three ringleaders in custody.

Maybe that was the end of it and Rick would be back with her by next shift. No chance she'd be that lucky.

The list of names was getting more focused, if not shorter. With little time and no resources, Sofie needed a new approach. She couldn't keep going out to interview people in hope of making a step forward. She needed to choose names that had the opportunity to skim inventory, and some vague but possible motive. The whole poisoning angle could be a distraction. Until she had confirmation from the autopsy, Sofie would concentrate on the meds. With luck this was a completely internal crime, because she wasn't going to get permission to interview anyone in the forward Temporaries.

She pulled all the potential names onto a single list. Selma Gold and Anna Kivi from the original list. Deva Lu was no longer a suspect; dying made him a victim. She hesitated, her finger holding the name on her pad. No. He could still be part of the meds conspiracy. His death might be coincidental — or might cause the med scheme to collapse.

The four new names Bindes gave her would need to be investigated. Rigby Collins: ran the lab where the Fades meds were manufactured, along with a number of other treatments for a wide range of conditions. He would have opportunity to manipulate the supplies. Elena Silva: med warehouse manager, definitely opportunity for her to skim large amounts. Blackfeather Huaman: reconciliation clerk. Sofie put a question mark where she'd been adding possible opportunity to the list of names. A clerk might have connections that would provide just the opportunity. And finally, Owen Shvets: distribution manager. Definitely had opportunity.

Motive would emerge from the interviews. And a little digging into their financial records, something Amanda was expert at doing. Six people were too many to track down on her own. Was it time to call for help? Sofie knew her reluctance to work with Amanda was personal and shouldn't affect the case, but Rick's social life was varied and expansive; he knew far more people than she did. She sent him a message. *Know anything about these people?* She listed the new names.

While she waited for the response, Sofie requested locations for all six names. Huaman, Gold, and Kivi were on shift. Silva and Collins were at home. Shvets was not located. He'd removed his tracker, was dead, or off-station.

"I see you are busy solving our latest mystery." Haadiya Rothwell. How the hell had he gained access to the room?

Sofie cleared the projection and turned the greet him. "Yes. Is there something I can help you with?"

His smile was probably supposed to be reassuring, but all Sofie felt was suspicion. Should she be looking in the Executive caste for her suspect?

"On the contrary," Haadiya said, "I was hoping to help you."

Unlikely.

"Do you have information?" Sofie asked, in case her first instinct was wrong.

"Before I tell you, I must ask a few questions. I would hate to waste your time with extraneous gossip. Are you sure that this illness is not simply bad luck? Working in Maintenance is dangerous, after all."

"It isn't only Maintenance workers. We can't be completely sure of anything until the case is solved," Sofie said. "Do you know something that would explain it beyond bad luck?"

"These violent protests, why are they not being dealt with?"

So nothing useful. He's warming me up for a favor. "I'm not assigned to the crowd dispersal team. Perhaps Captain Llewelyn could answer these questions."

He smiled again, but this time it seemed to say she'd won the round. If that was the case, he hadn't been trying hard. A token game so he could report he'd made the effort?

"If these illnesses are not a coincidence, then I may have information."

"I would appreciate anything you can tell me. It's not just illness. I'm sure you know a Support worker has died."

He glanced at the wall again. "If I could see your progress?"

"I am not allowed to share details of an ongoing case. If you get permission, I'm happy to share." Let Llewelyn deal with the politics. He took Rick away. He could deal with the consequences.

"Indeed. Then I will give you my news and hope it is not something you have already uncovered."

Sofie was sure he'd been sent so he could protect his employer, June Sato, the family Second. But maybe he had a personal agenda. "May I ask why someone so influential is willing to spare time to assist in an investigation?"

"The peace of the Mallet is vital to all. The families are worried that your case is the reason people are rising up. I'm surprised Nhu has not contacted you yet."

He might be guessing, but he was right that Nhu hadn't reached out after the first call. That would probably change if they found out about Haadiya's visit.

"Your information?" Sofie held up her pad ready to record the tip.

Haadiya put his hand on the pad. "No need to record this."

She put the pad on the table behind her.

"I know of two people who have reason to meddle with supplies. That is your avenue, right? Someone is reducing the effectiveness of medications?"

Sofie nodded.

"Both of these people have been spending credit that they shouldn't have. It's on the black market, so your research is unlikely to find it."

"Names?" The black market was all off-the-books, so pulling information meant you needed a mole inside their operation, and they were expensive, hard to identify, and often working more than one side.

"Elena Silva and Anna Kivi. Both women have opportunity to steal, and both are spending in the black market. Before you ask, I am not privy to the actual transactions."

"Thank you. That may speed up the case." Sofie would still need to follow up on the other names, but now she had two at the top of her list.

"It is my pleasure to help," Haadiya said as he left.

27

Sofie added Elena Silva's name to the list and requested background information. Anna Kivi was still at work, even this late in the day, so she could be interviewed while Sofie waited for a response.

The door to the case room opened. Sofie turned, ready to send whoever was intruding out before she increased the security level. Rick stood smiling at her.

"Are you back?" she asked. Having him with her for the interview would be perfect.

"Just regrouping with my team. I got your message." He nodded toward the wall. "Anything new?"

She told him about Haadiya's visit and the one new name.

"Don't know her." He pointed to the list of names. "I know Rigby and Blackfeather. They are not suspects."

"How can you be so sure?" Sofie struck out the two names, her question just curiosity. Rick wouldn't have vouched for them for no reason.

"I vet the people I sleep with." He grinned. "Thoroughly. And it was recent enough to still be good. What about the

Kivi woman? She keeps showing up, or am I reading that wrong?"

"No. She's my next interview, but I don't see anything about her life that points to too much credit or to a reason for blackmailing her into stealing. No kids, no family, no parents. Not many people who might be friends."

"How is it going alone?" Rick checked his pad.

"So far okay. I haven't been pulled off a lead to react to an emergency. I don't know how long that will last."

"I have to go," he said after checking his pad again. "If I can help, message me, but I'm patrolling the troubled areas. I won't be able to do much."

Sofie thanked him and then locked the door behind her so she could finish her plan without interruption. The request queue indicated she'd have her Silva report in five minutes. She could wait for that before heading out to Support.

She reviewed the notes from their original interview with Kivi that morning. The only impression she noted was that Kivi was lying. Rick thought so too. So she'd work on finding the lie this time.

The Elena Silva report appeared on her screen. Manager of the warehousing location for all meds before distribution. *Promising.* Sofie checked, and the meds were only in the warehouse for a short time. Some just passing through to the delivery service, others for a day, but nothing longer than that. Silva would have to work fast, but there was definitely opportunity.

Silva's personal finances showed a little more balance than her salary merited, but not enough to confirm she was the culprit. Her shopping habits were exactly what Sofie would expect for a Support employee of that level. Whatever she was doing on the black market wasn't funded by her salary. The report was no help, and showed no reason to prioritize the Silva interview ahead of Kivi. Sofie requested a report on the woman's movements in the last month and then packed her pad in a bag, checked her weapon, and headed out to Support.

The square outside the office was empty, which was almost as disturbing as the protest crowd earlier. Sofie checked for alerts and found a long list of offenses that could result in fines and jail terms. No curfew yet, but no one would risk increasing their debt by being on the streets and getting caught doing something a cop thought was suspicious.

She changed her notifications to provide an audible alert and pushed her earpiece in. She couldn't afford to miss any more updates.

S ofie used the directory to locate Kivi at her desk. Did she ever leave the building during work? Go to other locations?

If it didn't need to be someone inside the building... *Fuck. I've been looking at this all wrong.* The manipulation could be done by anyone with authorization codes. If the perpetrator had hacked in to bypass authorization, it could be anyone. And was likely to be someone in the dark streets. She'd been following her assumption that whoever was committing the crime must be part of the delivery process.

This was why she needed Rick. Doubt about current theories could hamstring an investigation. Talking through the new ideas and information kept the doubt under control.

She stopped following the highlighted path to think through the ramifications. No one had suggested a dark streets connection... except Rick. He'd suggested the meds were going to a criminal organization off-Mallet. The most logical contact for one off-station was the boss of the dark streets. She couldn't go into the dark streets alone to find the boss to interview him. And this was just an alternate theory. Anna Kivi or Elena Silva or someone she didn't yet know about could still be the mastermind.

Kivi's lie still needed uprooting. She wasn't at her desk now. The path was getting shorter; Kivi was coming toward her.

Anna Kivi turned a corner and came to a stop. "Detective?"

"I have more questions. Let's go back to your office."

The woman turned around and walked back the way she'd come. Sofie hurried to catch up while running questions in her mind.

"Would you like a stim-juice?" Kivi asked. "Our office mix is okay. I was headed out for a better choice when we ran into each other."

"I'm fine, thanks," Sofie said. "This probably won't take more than a few minutes." She didn't want Kivi out of her sight until the interview was over.

Kivi sat and clasped her hands on the desk. "Okay."

A ping sounded in Sofie's ear. "I need to get this," she said, holding up her pad. "Can't be off-line these days. The situation changes so rapidly."

The alert was her tracking report on Elena Silva. The analyst had added a comment at the top of the report. *No guarantee but this looks like the subject has a gambling problem. The most frequent stops are at what we have flagged as an off-the-books casino.*

Sofie glanced through the list of locations quickly. A gambling problem might explain why her credit balance wasn't out of order. An off-the-books casino meant no regulation and more scams than usual. Lots of fodder for the interview she'd be doing next.

"Your questions," Kivi said. "I am happy to assist, but my time is limited because my schedule is full."

Did the woman really think she was assisting? Sofie kept the thought to herself. The longer she could keep Kivi thinking she was a helper and not a suspect, the better.

"Your colleague, Deva Lu, is dead." Sofie looked for a reaction. She didn't expect tears, but even if she hated the man, a little sadness at the loss would be normal. Kivi's expression didn't change. And she was waiting for a question, not a statement. "Can you tell me about him?"

"I barely worked with him when he reported to me, and then he transferred. If you suspect him of a crime, I'm the last person to help you."

If this is the way she interacts with people, no wonder Lu transferred. "I'm often surprised by the details people don't even know they have. What kind of worker was he?"

"He did his job adequately." Kivi frowned, the first break in the barrier between them. "I don't know if he was intelligent enough, or committed enough, to advance. But I suppose if he was manipulating the inventory, he put his energy there."

A dead scapegoat is convenient.

Sofie let Kivi think Lu was the target of the investigation, so she would let her guard down. "Would he have had the opportunity?"

"I have no idea how a scheme like that would work, Detective."

"I'm sure you're intelligent enough to work it out," Sofie said. "Would *you* have the opportunity?"

"I wouldn't know how, so I can't say."

Sofie checked her pad. There was nothing there to help, but the woman was getting agitated now that the questions focused on her. "You are in a position of authority. That comes with a responsibility to ensure the security of the medical supplies, right?"

Anna Kivi shifted in her chair. "Are you accusing me of something?"

Sofie gave her fake reassuring smile. "We have to follow every clue. Please answer the question."

She pressed her lips together. Was it worry she'd been caught? Or anger at being confronted? "There are procedures. My training included checks and balances that would show the potential for embezzlement."

"And somehow you still have no idea if someone has the opportunity to commit a crime here. Interesting. It makes me think you got the job for reasons other than your ability."

That stung Kivi's ego. "I earned this position, Detective."

"I'm sure you did. If it was because of your intelligence or ability, you should be able to answer my questions."

Kivi's hands clenched. She'd missed the trap and stepped right into it. "I suppose someone might record false numbers." Her voice was tight. "Or work with a partner who diluted the effective ingredients. Or... I don't know off the top of my head."

Even if Kivi wasn't involved, she knew exactly how someone could get away with tampering with medical supplies. Still not enough to arrest her, but she was firmly at the top of the list now. "Why would someone do that?"

"That I can't answer, but you know life on the Mallet, Detective. Everyone has a reason to mess with the system."

Sofie checked her pad again. "I have another interview scheduled." Let Kivi stew over being dismissed.

She stood and walked away, sending the order to place a tracker on Kivi's movements. The next time she came, it would be with an arrest warrant.

29

Elena Silva was standing in the body of the warehouse when Sofie found her. A tiny woman, like a child wearing an adult's clothes. Her voice, strident with a veneer of whine, betrayed her innocent image as she issued orders to the people working around her.

Sofie showed her ID and suggested they talk in private.

"I can't leave," Silva said. "If I'm not here to keep them working, every single one of them would be gossiping and lying about. You! Those crates are ready to go."

"You must have an assistant," Sofie said. "It will only take a few minutes." The idea of trying to eliminate this woman as a suspect while she screamed at people around her made Sofie ready to throw her weight around.

"He's useless." Silva shouted out another order.

Sofie checked the information on her pad. "If you don't hand off the shift to Mr. Isaac in the next minute, I will bring you to the station and conduct my interview there."

Silva looked at her like she was impressed. "Fine."

The assistant took over, the space became quiet, and the

work continued. Sofie followed Silva to an office next to the entrance of the warehouse. The blinds dropped as soon as the door closed. The office was always in privacy mode when occupied. That didn't mean anything. Or it could mean something as innocent as the fact that Silva used her office for sex.

"What do you want from me?" Silva asked. She didn't offer stim-juice, or a seat, or anything that might extend the time she spent with Sofie.

"I'm investigating the recent increase in hospitalizations." No need to start with the potential murder. "We have indications that the supply records of certain medications are being falsified."

"Nothing to do with me," Silva said. "As far as my team is concerned, those crates could contain condoms."

"I find that hard to believe. Your job and this location are dedicated to medical supplies."

"Fine. Yes, we know it's medications, but it's all codes. We don't know exactly what is in there." Silva narrowed her eyes in what Sofie thought might be an effort to look legitimate. Or a dare to contradict her.

Sofie stared back at Silva, feeling juvenile but knowing if she played the same game, they would find some kind of common ground. "How do you know someone isn't setting you up to take the fall for something? If the contents of the crates aren't what's on the manifest?"

"Let them try. Every crate is sealed. The seal is checked when it comes in and when it goes out. That protects us from all kinds of finger-pointing."

If someone found a way to fake the seals, it would guarantee no one could prove tampering. "Has anyone tried?"

Silva laughed. "Never more than once. Look, sweetie, I

have real work to do. If you don't have anything else, I'll get back to it."

"Who applies the seals?" Before the crate was secured was the best time to skim some of the contents.

"Inventory. Any more questions?"

Sofie had lots of them, but she needed to do a bit of research before she confronted this woman again. If her abrasive personality was not a performance, she'd never be subtle enough for a long-term ongoing swindle like what was happening with the meds. "Not at this moment." She walked out just to piss off Silva, denying her the chance to throw her out.

30

Sofie didn't want to go back to the bullpen. The chance of being pulled off the case to deal with the protests — even temporarily — or of being trapped behind a mob was too high. What she really needed was more help, and that was not going to happen. She sent the request for a tracker on Silva, trying to decide which woman to follow.

She found a cafe, ordered stim-juice and a roast vegetable sandwich. When her order came, she took a pill with the first sip of her blufroot-flavored juice. The tang of the juice covered the faintly moldy taste of the sandwich. In a week she'd be done with hiding her medication. She'd resisted for so long, but now she was looking forward to the operation. Not that she'd have no more secrets to protect, but the biggest, nastiest one would be gone.

The approval of the two trackers came through. Sofie split her pad screen in three sections. One for Kivi, one for Silva, and one for updates on the crowd control efforts. The streets were quiet for now. And no new alerts from Llewelyn waited for her.

Silva's tracker pulsed in one place on the map overlay. She was at work. Her shift ended in two and a half hours, so if she left work before then, Sofie would follow up. If Sofie had a partner, one of them could go interview the workers while the other tailed Silva. *I need to stop wishing for the impossible.*

For now, keeping an eye on the tracker had to be enough.

Kivi, however, was on the move, coming toward the cafe. Sofie tossed her cup, plate, and napkin into the recycler and got ready to leave. Kivi's job required her to move around the section, so it could be innocent. But she was on shift and should be for another six hours. None of the legitimate work locations were in the direction the tracker was moving.

Sofie slipped out of the cafe and hurried to catch up with Kivi. The woman was focused on her path, so following would be straightforward. She was either going to the Administration section — she could have a valid reason for meeting someone there, including complaining about Sofie harassing her — or she was headed to the incoming Temporaries. That would be a problem. Hard to be stealthy if you had to pass a gatekeeper.

Kivi walked through the Administration blocks. It was more difficult for Sofie to hide now. Only a few people strolled the streets. There were few nooks to slip into if Kivi turned to look. Most of the entrances were flush with the walkway. There was no sense of urgency in this section. No hint that the station was on the brink of riots.

Kivi didn't check for tails. She simply focused on her destination. Not the Temporaries, but one of the outgoing distribution centers. She stopped at the first opening, waited for a mech truck to pass, and slipped inside.

Sofie walked up, peeked inside, and then stepped back

to avoid being bumped by the next mech truck. Kivi was talking to a man dressed in blue coveralls, and they were not happy with each other.

Sofie slipped inside and moved closer. It was too late to launch a drone, and the area was probably protected against them anyway. She turned on her pad to record and set it at highest sensitivity. Someone could clean it up later for evidence.

The lighting was dim; mech trucks didn't need brightness. Crates filled the back of the room, and a conveyor stalled as it waited for a metal container to be removed. The entire area was automated. Why was Kivi arguing with a technician? The man could only be there to service the equipment and debug any program glitches.

Sofie slid closer until she could catch their words.

"I said I was done," Kivi said. "If you want to keep going, get another partner. The cops are getting too close."

"You are fucking done when they say so," the man said.

He was in the shadows, which made it difficult for Sofie to identify him. It didn't matter; Kivi would give him up when questioned. No doubt of that in Sofie's mind. The more she heard and recorded right now, the better. And arresting Kivi would be easier when she was at her desk.

"You think I want to quit? I've got plans. If the cops weren't all over this, I'd still be building credit." Kivi dodged back as the man took a swing at her.

"Your plans don't mean a fucking thing. You get back to the job and keep the cops off our backs."

"Hit me, and someone will notice," Kivi said in a quiet, contained voice. "This is your fault. You got greedy."

"You think I won't dispose of you?" the man said. "No one will look for you. The cops will be distracted by the protests."

Sofie waited. She checked her pad and asked for rein-forcements. She couldn't arrest them on her own. Even if she waited for Kivi to be alone, it would be hard. And neither of them had said anything about meds. If she acted now, she might discover a completely different crime. Under normal circumstances, a free solve was a bonus, but today, only one crime mattered.

Her request for assistance was denied. The official reason was lack of available resources. Sofie interpreted that as everyone was on crowd control. Maybe the disturbances were some kind of master-plan. Keep the cops busy stamping out fires and commit a large-scale crime while no one is looking. She shook her head to dislodge the annoy-ance. There was no choice because the protests needed to be kept from exploding into riots.

Kivi wasn't talking. The man's last statement seemed to shock her out of the fight.

"Go back to your desk," he said. "No one is going to arrest you. Keep working for them and keep living. It's that simple."

"Fine." Kivi straightened her spine like she'd won the argument. "If this all falls apart, you are as fucked as me."

Sofie ducked into the office she'd been using as cover. Kivi marched past. When Sofie peeked around the doorway, the man was bending over a crate with a code scanner. She slipped out.

Anna Kivi wasn't in sight. Sofie messaged Llewelyn demanding a meeting as soon as she got back to the bullpen. She turned off the tracker on Silva. Whatever she was up to, it had nothing to do with finding the ringleader. Maybe Silva was a cog in the organization, but Kivi was the one to take down. Kivi was headed back to work. Sofie stopped watching the tracker.

The Mallet felt like it was thrumming. As she neared the bullpen, Sofie noticed more people in blue and orange. Not just buttons and badges, but also in their choice of clothes: blue overalls with orange shirts peeking through. The protests were gaining support. Nothing good would come of that. It wasn't illegal to wear colors outside your work shift. It wasn't illegal to walk around doing nothing. At least it wasn't illegal until a curfew was set. At that point it might be too late.

Llewelyn was in his office. Amanda looked up from her desk outside and nodded. When Sofie entered, Amanda walked in behind her and shut the door.

"You found the problem?" Llewelyn asked. "We might need you on the line soon."

"I have a good suspect," Sofie said. She gave him the details he needed to allow him to answer any questions from above. "I think I've eliminated my other possible suspect, but without help, I can only deal with one person."

"This Kivi woman was threatened? Why didn't you bring

her in for questioning?" Llewelyn checked the newsfeed on his wall screen.

"I was alone. And even if the people around or the man she was meeting didn't interfere, I wasn't sure I could escort her to the nearest transport." She tried not the let her frustration bleed into the words. It wasn't Llewelyn's fault she was working alone — or not totally his fault. "If I couldn't contain her, we'd lose our best chance to solve the case and calm the protests. I put a tracker on her."

"And the other woman?" Amanda asked. "I might be able to find time to check on her if you want confirmation either way."

Even Amanda's help would be better than no team at all. "If you have time, I have other things you might be able to help with."

"Let me remind you that I hand out the assignments here. I need Amanda right now. I need this case solved before things go completely off the rails and I have to pull you off, Sofie. That's how scared the Elites are. They'd rather let a murderer go than face a riot."

Like that hasn't happened before. "Okay," Sofie said. "But I won't hand you an innocent to take the fall. It's not how I work, and it won't solve the problem."

"I'm not there yet, but it might happen." He looked at the newsfeed again and shook his head. "I agree. Naming a scapegoat will only postpone the inevitable, but that might be enough for us to get back in control of the section."

Sofie got the message. Solve the case, or this Anna Kivi would take the fall no matter what. "Okay. I'll keep on her. My gut says she's the right person. I need to know the name of the guy in the receiving bay who threatened her. I'll go through the images of the staff; maybe we'll get lucky. I'll track him too if I get an identity. He's the link to the off-station perps."

"Don't waste your time," Llewelyn said. "I mean on following him. We can't do anything about what's happening off-station."

"He might be a contact between Kivi and whoever is benefiting. It won't take a second to find out," Amanda said. She held up her pad with five images displayed. "Which one is he?"

"The last one," Sofie said, thanking whoever decided that the work could be done with only a handful of humans.

"I'll keep an eye on the trackers," Amanda said. "It won't get in the way, and I'll let you know if Kivi meets with him again."

There'd probably be a price for Amanda's help later, but it lifted a weight off her shoulders. If Kivi wasn't their perp, then she couldn't afford to waste time on following up. "Thanks. I'll check with some of my contacts now that I have a name."

"Make it fast," Llewelyn said. "This crowd control stuff is costing us budget."

Sofie swallowed her response. He knew the case wasn't going to run on a timetable. He was telling her that if it wasn't solved today, it wouldn't matter. "Okay. Are you sure the protests will disappear if we give them a solved case?"

Llewelyn sighed as he took another look at the news-feeds. Sofie followed his gaze. The protests were scattered through the Maintenance section. It was going to be a challenge to get to Torque. The only real way for Kivi to avoid getting caught was to leave the Mallet. And Torque would know how.

"They are protesting the illness and now a poisoning. Any news on that aspect?"

Sofie shook her head. "Autopsy still not in." It wasn't delayed. It just felt like she'd been investigating for a week, not a little over two days.

"I can't guarantee it will stop it forever. We always live on the edge of violence. But it should slow them down while they look for another problem to chant about."

"I'll let Shehata know I'm heading through." She pushed up from the chair, automatically inventorying her body for Fades symptoms. The meds were working for now.

"We have a problem." Amanda looked up from her screen. "Kivi's tracker has gone dead."

32

If Anna Kivi was off-line, she could be dead. Or she had guessed she was being tracked and masked her chip. Not impossible to do, but a last resort for any sane resident of the Mallet. She'd need someone to turn it back on or she'd have no access to food, shelter, or work. All of which meant she would be dead soon. Support residents didn't have the skills to live in the margins. Although, Kivi wasn't the usual Support resident. She was working a big crime with off-Mallet connections. Not having a working tracker was a good way to avoid repercussions from her partners as well as getting arrested.

"If you don't need me, I'll go find her," Sofie said. "The other leads will just have to wait." If Llewelyn couldn't give her help now, she'd never get it.

"Be careful," he said. "Maybe get your armor on?" No offer of help.

Wearing riot gear would remind everyone she was a cop. No one would talk to Sofie if she looked ready to knock some heads together and arrest anyone in sight. And it could draw attention. The last thing she needed was to be a

cop alone in the middle of a crowd of dissatisfied Maintenance workers. "I'll be safe."

She went into the case room before heading out. She
uploaded everything from her pad to a private case directory and grabbed a second stunner. Two charged weapons
wouldn't look out of place. And they wouldn't offend
Torque.

She messaged Shehata that she'd be traversing Maintenance to the Temporaries and copied Rick. Shehata
responded with a suggested route to stay out of the worst
trouble. Rick just sent back *K*.

Outside, Sofie felt unease creep in. The square was
empty, but she could hear low chanting not far away. Like a
pot was getting ready to boil over; still savable if someone
acted fast.

She turned away from the noise and entered Maintenance. This wasn't her normal route, but it definitely looked
like a shortcut — one that didn't require her to go through
the dark streets. She set Shehata's recommended route and
let her pad point the way. As she passed side corridors, she
saw people. Sometimes they were squashed together,
blocking access to their location. Sometimes they were
moving. She stopped following the safe path long enough to
sneak down an alley and get a better look at the action. Yes,
people were moving toward a crowd. The chanting, origi-
nally low from individual voices, was gaining volume as the
number of participants increased.

Around the edge she noted cops standing elbow to
elbow. Some of the defenders were wearing the gray coveralls of the private security outfit from up front. Media
drones were circulating above the crowd.

She hoped Llewelyn was right about solving the case.

Even if he was, she had to move fast. If this crowd turned violent, no one would be able to stop them.

Shehata's route remained clear, and Sofie slipped into the Temporaries only a few minutes after witnessing the growing protest. No parties here. The streets and squares were empty until she was halfway through the section. Still no celebrations, but at least they weren't running for the outbound ships. Business would continue on the Mallet until someone blew it out of the system.

She slipped through the streets, peering into Torque's various haunts with no luck. She hoped he wasn't waiting for the next shuttle to safety.

33

Torque was at the bay when Sofie arrived. For the first time since she'd met him, he was working the floor, not just sitting back and issuing orders. The bay was busy, and there was a frantic air about the place. Maybe because people were moving fast, or because so many people were on shift.

He saw her and pointed to an office just inside the entrance. She waited for him to join her, not interested in interrupting the flow of people, only turning her chair to observe.

When she'd found the container of people waiting to be smuggled off-station in her last case, she'd identified the location by the different pattern of traffic. Today, workers entered and exited that bay in the same way as all the others. If Kivi was escaping the Mallet from this end, she wasn't doing it under Torque's eye. But there were more bays, and Torque wasn't the only one who managed illegal shipments.

"What can I do for you?" Torque walked past her and sat behind the desk. "You can see I'm busy, so make it fast."

"Is this busier than normal?" Sofie asked. If the bays were being emptied, were the Mallet's clients making a run for it? For good?

"We're still here, Sofie. I haven't had any evacuation orders. My company wouldn't leave any of us here if the situation started looking like it was getting out of control."

He truly believes they value him. Maybe they do. "So why are more ships going out? I'm right about that, aren't I? Your company is clearing inventory."

Torque nodded. "Yes, but it's not unusual. We do this every once in a while. If there's a big shipment of ore coming, we make space for the refined metals and slag."

The contracts were written to ensure the Mallet didn't become a slag pit. The station couldn't operate without room, so anything the Elites couldn't turn a profit on inside the Mallet was taken away with the refined product.

"And the private security up front? We don't have to worry that it's a takeover?" She didn't really care if one of the corporations took over from the Elites. Life couldn't get much worse.

"A precaution, as far as I know. Is that what you wanted to ask?"

"No. I have a case and I think you can help. Someone is stealing meds and messing with the expiry dates. The protesters found out. You've heard the chants."

"Tricky to do. Medical supplies are a locked-down system." Torque looked down at the floor, thinking. "Inside supply or from the imports?"

"Both. The thinking is if we catch the criminal, the protests stop for now."

"How many on your team?"

Sofie thought of lying, but she'd always been honest with Torque when she chose to answer his questions. "Me."

He pursed his lips, no longer thinking. He was assessing what he should say. Sofie had seen it before, every time he'd decided to tell her something. She waited.

Finally, he leaned forward, elbows on the desk. Keeping his voice low, he said, "Such a high-profile case should have more people. You think it's because someone doesn't want it solved? They want a riot?"

"A riot could destroy the Mallet." She couldn't quite ignore the suggestion, but she didn't want to give it life by agreeing.

"It's happened before, and the Mallet's still here," Torque said.

"Everyone else is keeping the lid on the protests. It's just bad timing for the case."

"Are you sure?" Torque asked.

"Are you sure about your information?" Sofie asked. She didn't like admitting she couldn't trust anything she had.

"Maybe not," Torque said. "My sources have been solid in the past, but we both know you can't rely on people staying loyal."

"It doesn't matter if you're right. I need to find the person responsible. I think they've started poisoning people to misdirect the investigation. I'm looking for someone in particular. Someone who was able to turn off her tracker."

"She's trying to get off-station?"

"I can't think of any other reason. I'm guessing her profits are held in off-station accounts, since we couldn't find any excess credits. She thinks we're closing in, so she leaves. We're stuck with a bunch of angry workers. The guy helping her might have to be the scapegoat. But he might be off-station himself."

She didn't tell him what she overheard in the front

Temporaries. Anna Kivi might be her perpetrator, but this scheme was run from some planet, or another station.

"I don't have anyone scheduled for extraction." Torque looked past Sofie's shoulder to the bay. "I can ask around. But if you find her, will you be able to bring her in? There are a lot of protesters between here and the jail."

"I'll be fine." Sofie counted on getting a team of officers to take the woman in. They could go back to riot duty when Kivi was safely locked up.

"You know why she would do this?" Torque asked as he typed on his pad.

"Credits," Sofie said. "Who are you contacting?"

"Need-to-know basis. I'll have your answer in a few minutes. So, do you know where the stolen meds are ending up?"

"Rick thinks maybe a new colony not on the approved list. Organized crime. There are not that many places that would need illegal drugs. The weird thing is some of the meds are for Mallet-based illnesses."

"There are easier ways to make credits," Torque said. "But you think maybe someone is setting up a place for Mallet refugees? Not a nice transition camp, but a new place to use them?"

"Slavery?" The people who worked the Maintenance and Manufacturing sections were close to that already. But there was always hope they'd find a way to buy out their debt. A slave was property. No way out.

"Anything is possible." Torque checked his pad. "No one is taking on escapees right now."

"You sure they aren't lying?"

"As sure as I usually am, so not completely."

Anna Kivi was still on the station. If she was stuck, Sofie

would find her. Even without her tracker, Kivi wouldn't be able to hide forever. Sofie wondered what was keeping her on the Mallet.

34

Sofie sent a message to Shehata again as she walked toward the entrance to the Temporaries, her mind turning over Anna Kivi's few options for survival off-line. There weren't many for a Support resident. They lived fairly stable lives with few opportunities to develop survival skills. Yes, she had been able to find ways to exploit the system, but that was mental work. The woman was unlikely to be able to figure out a place to sleep or a way to get food. Kivi's plans would all be short-term. And there was one place on the Mallet that people without a future went. Would she think of the dark streets? If she had enough credits, she could buy protection, but not forever.

Shehata acknowledged her message but there was no suggested route this time. She sent a text to Rick so he'd know where she was, and then stood inside the Temporaries trying to come up with a good reason for not looking into the dark streets. The last time she went in alone, she'd been attacked. But it hadn't stopped her from solving the case. And this time the rest of the Maintenance section was almost as dangerous.

Turning toward the dark street shadows, Sofie tapped both the stunners on her belt and loosened the closures on the straps. She would pull a weapon at the first sign of trouble. She doubted the protests had made it to this section, but there was always a chance.

There were guards at the entrance. Only three, but they were heavily armed and mean looking. If a crowd got too close, a few stunner shots would discourage the leaders.

"You want in, officer?" The man who spoke was tall and skinny. He had a scar across his cheek and a tattoo that followed the line, then turned into a skull.

"Detective," Sofie said. "Yes. I'm looking for a woman who might have fled here in the last hour. You know anyone like that?"

"Not telling you." This came from a short woman to his left. She was jumpy. If there was trouble coming, Sofie figured this woman could be the spark.

"Fine, I'll look myself." She took a step forward and the three guards shifted to form a barrier.

"The boss said everyone stays out," the man said.

The third guard was a boy. He looked about twelve and scared of everything, but trying to look cool.

Sofie turned to him. "The boss might be okay with me getting my suspect. Might stop all that." She tilted her head toward the sound of chanting.

The man elbowed the boy behind him, then said to Sofie, "Don't like to question orders."

Movement behind the guards caught Sofie's attention. Someone was approaching.

"Just yesterday he sent me a message to solve my case fast," she said. "You think your orders are more important?"

The movement resolved into a man wrapped in dark

gray cloak and scarf. Her messenger from yesterday. "Let her through."

The woman stepped aside and glared as Sofie passed. "Next time maybe you don't get your way," she muttered.

Sofie ignored the comment. She'd be angry too if someone undercut her authority without an apparent reason.

"You'll get to work faster this way," the messenger said.

"Did a woman come for sanctuary recently?" Sofie followed the man through the empty streets.

"We don't give sanctuary," he said. "This way."

"Where is everyone?"

"Safe."

"Did a woman from Support buy her way in?"

"If she was here, you'd have her already because the boss can smell real trouble when it comes in. I'm with you to guarantee safe passage since you can't manage that yourself."

So not everyone is welcome. "I don't need an escort."

She did feel better having one. Yes, she was armed and ready to protect herself this time. But it was better not to create a problem here.

"History proves otherwise."

Getting to the office faster was a benefit. If the protest crowds were confined to Maintenance, she'd be able to travel the rest of the Mallet without detours like this. And she would have to go through to Support because Anna Kivi, despite all expectations, must have found a way to hide close to home. "You think there's a reason everyone is so agitated?"

"People reach the end of their ropes. If enough people get there together, they lash out rather than kill themselves."

"Even here?" She gestured around her to include the entire dark street area.

"The boss keeps an eye on the weak ones. They don't get a chance to make trouble."

Meaning they died, one way or another. "We'll break this up," Sofie said. "Things will settle again."

They were almost at the end of the road. She could see the street ahead was clear, so she'd be in the case room in a few minutes.

Her guide stopped and took her elbow to stop her leaving. "Things won't settle for long. Something is different this time." His eyes locked on hers.

"Is this another message from the boss?" Her gut told her this was important. This man lived in a different world from the rest of the people on the Mallet. He had a completely different way of looking at life. And maybe that was the problem. Without a sounding board, she couldn't look beyond her own assumptions.

"Everything I say and do comes from the boss."

"Why is this different?"

"Someone is stoking a fire. Someone powerful is forcing change. They won't give up. Don't let the Mallet die to stop them."

"Who?"

He let go of her elbow and spun away. She watched him turn into the first side street and knew there was no point in running after him. He knew where to hide; he knew how to evade. This was his home turf.

She thought about her unanswered question. Who? Elites wouldn't want anarchy because it would affect their profits. Just like the boss of the dark streets, they wanted a stable — if miserable — Mallet.

Off-station? She had no idea who could benefit from the Mallet's destruction. Maybe destruction wasn't the goal.

.

35

T he autopsy results were in by the time Sofie
returned to the case room. She put her stunners
on the charger and pulled up the report.

The top of the file had a stamp across it. INCONCLU-
SIVE. *Great. Another useless dead end.* Sofie kept reading,
hoping that the medical definition was different from hers.
And in her experience what wasn't there could be more
helpful than what was.

The cause of death in each case was organ failure, which
didn't mean anything other than they couldn't pinpoint
what made the organs fail. Cause of death was the inconclu-
sive part. So, no one was able to say whether it was natural,
accidental, suicide, or homicide. Leaving the cause unre-
solved allowed Sofie to keep investigating, so it was better
than a conclusion of natural causes, which wouldn't do
anything to calm the protests.

It wasn't the first time she had to dig deeper into an
autopsy report to draw her own conclusions. All the bodies
had chronic conditions — one of them had been undiag-

nosed until they cut him open. All had traces of poison in their systems, but in small enough quantities that it could have been environmental. The only thing that piqued the interest of the medical examiner was the low level of the legitimate medications.

Sofie grabbed her pad and called the number in the contact field.

"Medical examiner's office."

"I need to speak to the person who did the recent autopsies requested by Doctor Petra Starlight." He'd know she was police from the ID on the caller code.

"What do you need to talk to me about?"

"Would the low levels of the medications have contributed to the deaths?"

"It is possible in a number of ways. I wasn't informed I needed to do more complex testing."

If he thought she was blaming him, Sofie wouldn't get anywhere. "I know. It's just something I thought of as I read. You have low levels of medications, so the chronic conditions would be worse, right? And then a little poison might have more effect."

"I tested the medications Doctor Starlight sent along. Every one of them was stale. Still enough to manage the condition if the problem was temporary. But depending on how long the dose was altered, maybe a cause for concern."

She needed him to be more specific, and he was doing his best to avoid specifics. Sofie wondered if there was a point in knowing the answers. Anna Kivi was her culprit. Catching her was priority number one. But... the deaths might point to a motive, or a conspiracy. Torque's words about off-station influence came back to her. "Okay. I guess there's nothing here to help my case."

"Wait," he said.

Good, he wanted to help now. Her tone had reminded him that it wasn't just a box to check on a report. Somehow, he'd forgotten that there was a potential murder case.

"Okay," he said moments later. "Give me a minute to research."

Sofie put the pad on speaker and started repacking her gear for a search. Alone it would be difficult, but not impossible. She had to be fast, but one person could move faster than two. No arguments about a plan — of course, no way to question the validity of her plan.

"Okay. I have something that might help. Two of the patients had the same condition. One, let's call him A, was being treated and the other, B, was undiagnosed. A and B are both male so we can rely on the comparisons more than if they were not of the same sex. No hormonal complexity, you understand."

Sofie pulled out the autopsy matrix. The two patients were easy to find. If the medical examiner wanted to pay lip service to patient privacy by not using names, it didn't make any difference to her. "Okay."

"The undiagnosed patient would have symptoms, but for this condition those are usually mild and manageable. And the person being treated would suffer the same inconveniences because their dose was too low. Why would someone put up with even mild symptoms when they should not be experiencing any?"

"Good question. Do you have an answer?"

"No. But both of these patients would have reacted more severely to environmental poisons than a healthy person. If your suspect knew this, and you could prove it, I would change the manner of death to homicide."

It was a weak connection, but homicide included accidental deaths during the commission of a crime. And would her suspect know about the poison affecting these two patients more than the average Mallet resident? Probably. "It does help, thank you. What about the other patients?"

"I would say that if two of the deaths are ruled homicide, we should look closer at the others. And someone should be checking every dose of the various treatments to ensure they are the correct potency. Too little may be causing inconveniences, but for some conditions, too strong is lethal."

Sofie touched the medications in her pocket. Only a few more days before she got the operation. If the Mallet still existed at the end of the week.

"Does Doctor Starlight know about that recommendation? It wasn't in the report." Sofie checked the newsfeeds as she spoke. Time to head out of the safety of this room and find Kivi.

"It will be added. I will send an alert to all medical professionals to be aware of the problem. Do you think solving your case will bring an end to the tampering?"

Sofie paused. She didn't want to give the man an automatic response that everything would be fine. It wouldn't. "I don't know. It will stop one person, but if there are more, we don't know."

"Well, I will say my prayers to the universe that you are successful."

Sofie figured actions were more effective than prayers. And now she really needed help. The protests would get in her way and, despite the benefits of going solo, she couldn't waste time second-guessing what she found.

Llewelyn had enough on his mind, so she sent a message to Amanda asking for Rick to be reassigned.

Can't take him off crowd management. I'll be there in five minutes with my gear ready.

Sofie reminded herself that Amanda was a first-rate detective and the case was more important than her own feelings.

She checked to see if Kivi's tracker had turned back on. No.

36

"Where do you want to start?" Amanda asked as she changed into civilian clothes.

"She wasn't in the dark streets, Temporaries, or Maintenance a half hour ago," Sofie answered, slipping on a hooded jacket. "She knows Support, so she's most likely to be there."

She tucked her stunners onto the belt under the jacket. No sign of anything like a uniform or official gear meant they could slip through the section without notice. Speed was their edge now. And the disguise would be enough to keep them from being dragged into crowd control if the problem had spread past Maintenance.

"Then we start searching around her office or her home?" Amanda motioned for Sofie to pull the hem of her hoodie down a bit more. "I'd think home first."

"I've got a request in for a search warrant on the office and home." Sofie pushed open the door and led Amanda out.

The streets outside were getting more crowded but no

one seemed to be organizing into a mob. As they passed through to Support, there were fewer people gathered. Sofie remembered to let Shehata know where she was going and then took the fastest route to Kivi's home neighborhood.

Like most of the Mallet, the area around Kivi's address contained cafes, small stores, a few bars, and stim-juice stands.

"Split up and cover the ground faster?" Amanda suggested. "You have a picture of her?"

Sofie sent an image to Amanda's pad. "Can you speed up the warrant process?"

"Already did. Probably an hour, maybe less. Everything is slow because of the protests. Arrests bogging down the court. Most of us are on crowd control. If I was inclined toward crime, I'd be busy."

Amanda took off to the left and Sofie walked to the first store on her right. A small grocery — apparently people in Support had room at home to cook. She pulled out her police ID and brought up the picture of Kivi.

"Hi, I'm looking for this person," she said, holding both items out to the clerk behind the checkout scanner. "When was the last time you saw her?"

"What makes you think I seen her?" The clerk nodded toward the image.

Sofie looked at him and raised her eyebrow. He might be used to dodging questions for any number of reasons, but he gave off an air of familiarity with police. Where did Support get workers for these jobs? He looked about fifteen. Not one of the kids who lived here. They were mostly slated for teaching positions or higher despite the supposed equal-opportunity assignments on the Mallet. Not a regular Main-tenance kid either — they were too rough around the edges to serve the refined Support residents.

She should have researched this before coming to the store. Normally she would have his name and background memorized. Being without a partner was pushing her to carelessness.

If he felt threatened, he might be more cooperative. "Who hired you to work this counter?"

"Same as everyone around here. I didn't score high enough for a regular Executive position. Yeah, my dad is the chief of the media relations group, but I get to sell crap."

Unless you worked with Support on a regular basis, it was easy to forget that the only people on the Mallet with a guarantee for their kids were the Elite and Executive. No matter how stupid or arrogant or defective their kids were, they were family. Everyone else went into the pool and were assigned as needed.

"So have you seen her?" Sofie held up the picture again. "She lives around the corner."

He glanced down at her pad. "Yeah. She doesn't usually buy much. Not a cook, I guess. She was here this morning. Bought a bunch of premades. She in trouble?"

The purchase would show up on the financials when Sofie got access to the details. But her tracker didn't show her coming to this location. "When?"

He pulled up the records on the scanner pad. "Yeah, about an hour ago."

After she'd deactivated her chip. "How did she pay?"

"Yeah, credit chips. Not usual, but sometimes happens when customers are trying to keep a purchase hidden from a partner. Like a surprise, or something."

A stash of credits would make sense, and explain why Kivi didn't seem to have a suspicious balance in her account. It was going to make their search harder if she was buying things with credit chips. "How many premades?"

He looked at the pad again. "Like enough for three days if that's all she's eating, and she isn't skipping."

Kivi had enough food to survive off-line for a few days. She was smart. By then, everyone might be tied up in the struggle to keep the Mallet running. She'd be long gone by the time Sofie could get the investigation restarted.

"Okay, thanks," Sofie said. She headed out of the store.

"Hey, am I in trouble?"

Sofie kept walking. It would do him good to worry for a while.

The next place was a stim-juice bar. Nobody there knew Anna Kivi. The next, a clothing place where she'd bought some warm jackets with credits. Then Sofie was done and waiting for Amanda on the street.

Amanda turned the corner and joined her a minute later. "Clothes and food. She's stocking up. Somewhere cold and hidden. Three days."

"Same here. So up to six days total. Paid with credit chips. But where? I mean, if she's planning to get off the Mallet, she needs to be near the Temporaries. My contact on the outbound hasn't seen her. And the front is controlled by a private security company."

Amanda peeked at her pad. "If she's working with the right people off-station, she would get through the front Temporaries. And maybe your contact isn't the only one who smuggles people for a fee."

Why did she have to add that last bit? Like I didn't know.

"You know where else would be cold enough for her to need a jacket?"

Amanda grinned. "Her home. No chip means she's not assigned to the quarters. No utilities."

The risk of a mech coming by to clean or a new resident

moving in was high, but it wasn't unusual for that process to take a week. And with the protests? Well, everything is back-logged, right? "We need that warrant."

37

The warrant arrived as Sofie and Amanda approached Kivi's office building. There were two stim-juice bars and a small grocery on the square.

"We should check to see if she did any stocking up from here," Amanda said. "If she's got more supplies than we thought, our plans need to change."

"Go ahead, but be quick," Sofie said. Amanda had a point, but Sofie wanted to act on the warrant. It wouldn't take two of them to check one store.

Amanda joined her two minutes later. "No. So we have her timeline right."

"I'm not sure her timeline will make a difference," Sofie said, leading Amanda toward Kivi's workspace. "These protests are controlling everyone's schedule. If she's planning on going through the front Temporaries, her escape route may be cut off as the Elites flee."

"What do you think we'll find in the office?" Amanda asked. "She can't be hiding out here."

Sofie stifled a sigh. Rick never asked her stupid questions. "We still need some kind of proof of her crimes. She's not going anywhere this second, but someone will clear out her office at some point."

"Her home, too," Amanda said.

Like I hadn't thought of that.

When they reached Kivi's workspace, Amanda overrode the security and started opening files on the pad while Sofie looked at printouts. Hard copies were unusual, but not so rare they rang any alarms. The contents looked like a list of medications with amounts and dates. "Is this in the network?" She showed it to Amanda.

"There's a file with that name, but it's not the same one." She flicked the wall screen on and pointed at the projected document. "Not even about meds."

Kivi must have left in a hurry. Leaving evidence like this lying around was a mistake. "Okay. We'll seal the office and let someone analyze what the fuck was going on later."

Amanda typed a command into the pad and Sofie's ears popped as a security field slid into place. A holo projected the crime scene warning.

"Her home?" Sofie asked. "I don't think she'll be there, but if she's this careless at the office, we might find a clue to her hiding place."

"True. I think we should take the time to look at the details of her financial records now that we have access. If it looks too complex, I'll check on it later, but there could be a trail."

Sofie sat at the desk and waited for Amanda to do her snooping. If Kivi had left a financial clue about where she was hiding, the delay would be worth it. And if she wasn't at home, and hadn't left a clue, the only option left was to walk the Mallet hoping for a bit of luck. She'd set a facial recognition scan to find Kivi an hour ago, but there were no results yet. Kivi would be smart enough to avoid cameras, so it was a long shot.

"She emptied her accounts yesterday," Amanda said. "Some in credit chips, enough to cover the purchases and passage off the Mallet. The rest transferred to a bank on C'koo. They keep financial records secret. I've never heard of anyone getting information from there. And it means she didn't have to wait around while the money was transferred."

The Mallet had no influence off-station without a client corporation to help. And even if one of them agreed, it would take too much time. "How much for the ticket out of here?" Sofie asked. Since travel away from the Mallet was restricted, there were no standard prices. People left on business and the Mallet paid. No one left on vacation.

"By my calculations, around fifty thousand." Amanda looked up from the screen. "You think that's right?"

It was a lot of credit. Sofie checked her notes on Kivi's salary. "If she had that much ready to be liquidated, she hasn't been using her salary for day-to-day. Any chance you can find another account?"

"She probably has multiple ones in different names. It's going to take a while. Although she should have used her salary for expenses. Stupid to dip into her illicit funds." Amanda typed in a query sequence then closed her pad. "I'll get an alert if anything shows up."

Sofie flicked through the information on Kivi's finances she'd pulled earlier. "I should have noticed the balance was too high."

"It's not that far out of the ordinary," Amanda said. "I don't think she was dipping into the credits from the meds thing. Those funds were probably on C'koo all along. She has another small side gig, I'm sure."

If that was true, it might link to Kivi's location. "We don't have time to figure out what other crimes she's committing. Let's go check out her home."

Amanda closed down Kivi's screen and checked her own pad. "Protests are boiling over again. We need to be alert."

"In Support?" Sofie pulled out her own pad. "Not yet. But the crowds are building around the entrances."

Amanda stepped through the security screen and disappeared from Sofie's view. Sofie looked around the office space one more time. It wasn't really an office, more a workstation. No privacy normally. So how had Kivi managed to run a complex scam from here?

She has another office.

SOFIE CAUGHT UP WITH AMANDA. "Can you find out if she's renting another space?"

Amanda grinned at Sofie and then opened her pad. She started typing as she walked. "There are only a few spaces available that haven't been assigned for shops or residences. It does make sense. And you think we'll find her hiding out there if she has one?"

"It would be perfect. A small office would have a toilet. No shower, but she isn't planning to be there long. It would have heat and light."

Amanda stuck her pad into her pocket. "I've requested an inventory of all spaces that can be rented and the names of the tenants. I asked for a separate query on vacant ones. We can check the ones that should be vacant after we go through her quarters if the query doesn't hit with an obvious place."

· · ·

ANNA KIVI'S home was empty. Not only of Anna, but of anything not bolted down. The dust on every surface told Sofie it hadn't happened in the last day or two.

38

"She was already running when you first questioned her," Amanda said as she looked in the kitchen cupboards, the only place where Kivi might have forgotten something.

Sofie ran a finger through the dust on the countertop. "At least five days," she said. "Before we even knew there was a problem. Before the protests started."

Maybe she set up her escape plan when the scheme began. If Sofie's own meds were a reliable example, this had been going on for less than a month. Or the tipping point happened within that time. If Kivi had managed to be careful, the scam could have been going on for years.

"We definitely need to find her hideaway." Amanda closed the cupboards and peeked in the bathroom. "Nothing here either."

Sofie sent a message to the crime scene team to process the quarters. Low priority because Kivi had cleaned the place out. "Any result on your search of available spaces?"

Amanda checked her pad. "There are a few in the area. Why wouldn't it show on your track of her activities?"

There were a lot of reasons, including that Kivi had someone edit the records. "Would you be able to tell if the records were altered?"

"We need to get back to the bullpen for that," Amanda said. "Did you think to check all her travels?"

Sofie ignored the jab at her competence because this time Amanda hit home. She hadn't done a detailed analysis. Had she missed anything else? Not having support was no excuse if she missed something critical. "It's worth another look. Any ideas for our next steps other than go back and review everything I've pulled together to date?"

"No."

Sofie secured Kivi's quarters before they headed back to the station. Every time she went back, she worried that the protests would stop her leaving. Or she'd be reassigned. Her grace period was running out and priorities would change.

She scanned the street, hoping for inspiration. "What if one of the places she goes to legitimately is also her hideaway?"

"Like someone has a back room they let her hide in?" Amanda followed Sofie's gaze. "Only a few are big enough to have a stock room."

Sofie's pad pinged with an incoming call. She checked the ID. Doctor Petra Starlight.

"There are new patients," Petra said, not waiting for Sofie's greeting.

"How many?" Sofie gestured for Amanda to stay with her.

"Two, but they are not Maintenance workers. We have a judge who's comatose, and an Elite."

"Why would an Elite go to a Support clinic?" she asked Petra.

"You're thinking we might have more people up there that we don't know about?" Petra asked.

"I wasn't thinking that, but it's possible. Why did this Elite come to you?"

"I issued a quarantine alert. I should have told you, but it was the only way I could find out if this affected the Elites. No one on the Mallet will ignore something like that. And we have a few private rooms fit for Elites."

"Who is it?" Sofie asked.

"Juliette Mabior. She's an artist."

"Is she able to answer some questions?"

"No medical reason she couldn't," Petra said.

"Okay. I'll be there soon." Sofie ended the call and filled in the blanks for Amanda.

"Should we split up?" Amanda asked. "I can go to the stores that might have room for someone to hide."

Sofie weighed the options. If they split up, Amanda could eliminate possible hiding places near Kivi's home. Interviewing Mabior wouldn't take two people. But if they split up, it meant each of them traveling the streets alone. The protests were growing, according to the most recent alerts. "We stick together. Let's close the loop on the locations here. Then we both head to the clinic."

Amanda led the way to the grocery. The clerk at the front was less cooperative than earlier, but the back room was empty except for a few crates lined up against the wall.

"Stocks are getting low," the clerk said. "Deliveries can't get through."

The same result in the cafe. No place for Kivi to hide.

39

Petra was waiting in reception when they arrived. Sofie introduced Amanda and followed Petra down a different corridor than usual to a private room.

"I am not willing to discuss my condition," Mabior said before Sofie could form her first question.

"This is a criminal matter," Sofie said. "I apologize for the inconvenience. Your help would be most valuable."

"It is bad enough that I must recover in such poor surroundings. I will not justify myself to anyone. I have provided the doctor with what she needs. My own personal physician will be here to facilitate my transfer to a better clinic any moment."

This was not Sofie's strength. Talking to someone with the ability to have her terminated on a whim was hard enough. Convincing her to assist might be impossible. Amanda's political skills were about to become an asset. Sofie nodded to her to take control of the interview.

"Would you be amenable to Doctor Starlight sharing what she knows?" Amanda asked. "We all want to ensure your situation improves."

Mabior flicked a glance at Petra and then rolled her eyes. "She may. The Mallet is becoming chaotic, and if I can help to bring back the peace and stability we all enjoyed before this, I will." She laid back in the bed and closed her eyes.

Petra drew them back to the corridor. "Her doctor will not be transferring her out," she said. "Her Pratham ordered her here. I'm not sure if she knows that, but we'll keep her until we are sure it's safe."

"Are you treating her?" Sofie asked. "I mean, she's going to take you away from the other patients."

"Her doctor is on his way, but he'll treat her here and will share all the information he gathers."

If they were wrong and this was the start of some new illness, it wouldn't matter. "So what's her story?"

Amanda held out her pad to record the answer.

"Same as everyone else. She has a condition, and the treatment is failing. Genetic conditions don't play by our rules. The Elites try to eliminate these things through selective breeding, but it's not possible to do so completely. The judge bothers me more. His records show no underlying problems."

"Will you keep us updated as you find more?" Sofie asked. The judge worried her too.

"Of course," Petra said. "I don't like losing patients, and if someone made this happen on purpose, I want them caught."

Sofie thanked her and made to leave.

"One more thing," Petra said. "Our ward is full. I've been given authority to manage other clinics in this situation, but the patients will be spread across the Support section."

The change could mean missing patterns in the illness. "Let's hope we get this under control soon." Sofie nodded to Petra and then left the clinic.

40

"Where next?" Amanda asked as they exited the clinic. "The list of units? If we find Kivi fast, we can get her into a cell and then it doesn't matter if the protests turn violent."

Before Sofie could answer, her pad beeped. She wished she could ignore it, and normally would during a hunt. This time it was an all-force alert, and Amanda was already reading it.

"We're supposed to get our riot gear on," Sofie said before Amanda could point it out. It was petty to feel a little triumph in it, but Sofie needed a win no matter how small.

"We'll lose our target," Amanda said. She didn't move to comply with the order.

Disobeying a direct order would get them a reprimand. If they brought Kivi in and she was behind the crime, their disobedience would be forgotten. If they failed or got hurt, they might find themselves demoted. The risk was worth it to Sofie. What surprised her was Amanda's reaction.

"I'm not stopping. You don't have to come with me," Sofie said.

Amanda shook her head. "Thanks for not saying Rick would keep going. What's your plan for not getting trapped in a riot?"

"Thanks for assuming I have one. I'll let Rick know where we are. He'll give us a heads-up if the action is headed toward us. We run or hide depending on the situation."

"Good enough." Amanda checked her pad. Sofie saw a list of unit numbers. The addresses flickered, then aligned over a map of the Mallet. "If we assume she's leaving the station, she's not likely to hide too far from the outgoing Temps. Unless we really think the front smuggles people out?"

It was likely they did under normal circumstances, but with a private security team on duty, Sofie figured those activities had shut down or shifted to Torque's domain.

"Good assumption." Sofie told Amanda about her encounter at the front. "I believe my contact when he says he isn't involved, but he's not the only player."

"We'll find out who else is involved when we need to," Amanda said. "If we start searching units around Kivi's home and move toward the outbound Temporaries, we'll find her or herd her."

Sofie sent a message to Rick, putting the plan to him for input.

He answered immediately. *Accept the tracking link I sent, and I'll keep an eye open for danger. I'll update you when I see you get close to the Temporaries. You'll be safe enough when you get inside.*

Sofie hit the approval and then looked to Amanda. "We should stick together."

Amanda looked toward the side streets as if planning a route. "Okay, follow me."

. . .

THE FIRST TWO units were still unoccupied, which matched their official records. The third was a small unit tucked into the space between a stim-juice stand and a specialty tea store at the edge of the Support section.

"It looks like it was intended as a storage space for the businesses next door." Sofie touched the pad with her ID card to override any security. The door popped on its hinge but stayed closed. "Shouldn't take long."

She pushed open the door, expecting the lights to come on automatically as they did in most units. No luck, and Sofie didn't want to feel inside for a switch. If this was Kivi's hiding place, she would contaminate any trace evidence by pawing at the walls. She held up her pad and used the light from the screen to illuminate the space.

It was half the size she expected. A room only about one meter by two meters. No services for the tenant, no light switch, no entertainment unit, no bathroom. Against the far wall, Sofie spotted a bundle of blankets and empty packages from auto-heating meals.

"I'll notify the crime scene team," Amanda said. "Don't even go inside. There are no clues in the open. She's gone."

"From here at least." Sofie took some photos without violating the scene. Then she set a police barrier and pulled the door shut. "We need to keep going. She can't have relied only on this one."

Amanda checked the map. "You think she moved closer to the Temporaries, or she's left the station?"

"You know as much as I do," Sofie said, but this time she didn't feel any resentment. Maybe Amanda was growing on her. "If we're going closer to the protests, let me check with Rick."

Amanda flicked through her own pad while Sofie called Rick. This time she needed a conversation, not a message.

"Busy right now," Rick said. "Make it fast."

Sofie heard shouting in the background. "We're thinking of heading toward Torque."

"Can you wait an hour? We'll have this under control soon, but you might not want to walk through right after we arrest a handful of random people."

"Okay. Call me when it's safe enough."

She turned to Amanda. It wasn't a great time to delay following Kivi, but this was a consequence of choosing not to grab their riot gear. "We could go into the office, pick up our gear."

"And get pulled into some suppressing action? Or processing arrests?" Amanda held up her pad. The map was gone, replaced by a list of addresses and names. "Or we could go talking to the families of our new patients."

It was a smart thing to do. She'd already accepted the reality of avoiding the protests. It was frustrating to be pulled away from a good lead, but it was only for an hour. And Kivi would be stuck too. More than Sofie and Amanda, because she didn't have someone feeding her information. The woman was either with her contact in the Temporaries, or she was holed up, waiting out the protests.

"The Elite or the judge?" Sofie asked. Maybe Amanda could talk her way into an interview with the Mabior family. "Either way, it's not a great idea to stand out here while you make the calls." She led the way to the stim-juice bar. There were only two tables inside, but both were empty. Sofie bought them drinks and joined Amanda at the farthest table from the entrance.

"The judge's family won't resist, or if they try, we have the authority to compel them," Amanda said, continuing the discussion. "But I think we should try out the Mabior family first. The Second should be amenable, and maybe he can instruct the patient to cooperate."

"Send me the map while you try to get us an appointment."

Sofie opened the map and stared at the locations, hoping for some hint she could use to narrow down the possibilities. Only one place on the map could be dismissed. It was used as a gathering place for the local Accept protectors. Kivi would never be willing to sit through their lectures or pretend to follow the basic tenets of the belief. Accepting her fate was the last thing she would do.

41

The Mabior Second was a man young enough to be Sofie's son, not that she ever planned to have a kid and subject it to life on the Mallet. She watched over Amanda's shoulder to avoid being seen as Amanda spoke to him through the pad. Not exactly hiding, but she didn't want to be drawn in if the Second wanted to avoid their questions.

"I understand, Detective," the man said. "You feel that there is some kind of link between the unrest of the lower classes and the illnesses."

"It would be valuable to our investigation to be able to speak to Madam Mabior," Amanda said. "It is odd to have such a prominent and successful artist fall ill, and even more so to find her in a Support clinic."

"Juliette is talented and usually in excellent health. We moved her to the clinic to comply with a health order."

Sofie figured it was more to do with getting sickness away from the Elite section. She pressed her lips together to stop herself from joining the conversation.

"Admirable of your family," Amanda said. "Would the Pratham be willing to encourage her to speak with us?"

The face on the screen hardened at the suggestion. Sofie hoped the rumors were untrue about the Mabior Pratham. She'd heard more than a few stories about his temper. Anyone who attempted to persuade him to do anything he didn't want to was in danger of demotion. There was no question of if he would take offense; he always did. He was always right. If he liked someone, they were never wrong — unless they disagreed with him. He had no real loyalties beyond the family bottom line.

"The Pratham will not interfere with a family member's private choices." The words were pinched out. Perhaps this Second had experienced the reality of the gossip. "If Juliette is not willing to speak to you, no one will force her to do so. It is not illegal to hold your own health details confidential."

This was far more resistance than Sofie was used to. Nhu would have found a way to help, Haadiya too. The thought of the two liaisons gave her pause. They had been absent. It had been three days since the case opened, and there was no direct Ruiz or Sato involvement. Surely Haadiya would drop in more than twice to find out what was happening, if only to hold anything he learned as leverage for a future transaction. But Llewelyn said he was dealing with all the interference, so maybe he was answering their questions.

"As you wish," Amanda said. "If it becomes a legal issue, should I contact you first? Or the Pratham's aide?"

The man's eyes narrowed. He was assessing the political implications of passing the problem up the line to the aide versus handling the problem himself. It didn't take long for him to come to a decision. "Of course, it will be better to reach out to the aide. They have the Pratham's ear."

Amanda thanked him and ended the call. She drank

half of her stim-juice before she started talking. "There's something wrong in that family. He was willing to forfeit what could be valuable information. That Pratham must be a nightmare."

"That's his reputation," Sofie said. "It won't end up being a legal issue, though. If the illness gets that far, we'll have a lot more patients to interview, ones who'll be easier to access. So let's try the judge's family."

THE JUDGE'S family was happy to talk to the police. Their home was in the Authority section, next to Support. A brisk ten-minute walk later, Sofie and Amanda were sitting with the judge's wife, drinking tea and making small talk to warm her up to the questions they hoped would solve the case.

"So, Detectives, what can I do to help you?" Mrs. Veltosh said. "My husband is very ill, and I'm sure the doctor knows much more about his condition than I do."

Sofie nodded to Amanda to take notes. "Our case is about the reason so many people are falling ill," she said. "Most have underlying issues that are not being treated as effectively as expected. Your husband has no chronic conditions, as far as his doctors are aware."

Mrs. Veltosh looked down at her hands. They were cradling the fine china cup gently. Sofie didn't see any trembling or tightness. The woman's posture was still perfect, and not a line or blush marred her face. Regardless, regret and fear radiated from her like a stink.

She took a deep breath and looked back at Sofie. "He has a condition. We hid it from the authorities. It's not illegal to do so."

That's not necessarily true.

"What condition?" Sofie asked, keeping her voice level to

avoid sounding judgmental. The woman was right, but if he needed his meds like she needed hers, it could be construed as a crime to obtain them outside the normal process. If the condition was like the Fades, it would be illegal to conceal it. If it was benign, perhaps a judge would know more about the legality.

If Bindes wasn't supplying Authority, he might know who provided black market medication to this section of the Mallet.

"He was diagnosed with Dashard syndrome as a child. His parents covered up the records and kept him healthy with off-market pills."

Dashard syndrome was deadly if not properly treated. Without the right meds, the judge would be dead in a couple of days. And calling his meds off-market didn't mean they were legitimate. He'd been taking a huge risk with his life. "Dr. Starlight needs to know about the Dashard. Will you contact her, or would you prefer we take care of it?"

Mrs. Veltosh relaxed in the same invisible way she'd been radiating fear and regret. "I will do so when you leave."

"Why did he feel the need to hide it?" Amanda asked.

Of course, she's perfect so has no idea why anyone would need to protect themselves from scrutiny.

"His job." Mrs. Veltosh put the cup on the table. "He works on highly complex corporate contracts. If they found out he was less than healthy, he would be presiding over aggravated assault and malingering cases. At least that's what he told me. I wish we'd been completely honest from the beginning. We would still be comfortable. We'd still live in this neighborhood."

Sofie didn't bother to engage in spinning what-might-have-been stories. "Call Dr. Starlight as soon as possible. It might save his life."

42

Outside on the street, Sofie sent a message to Rick and waited for a response. "We've got no choice but to go into Maintenance," she said to Amanda.

Finding Kivi now was their only way to go. She didn't care if the protests were cleared or not. She needed a path through to the two addresses on the list. Both were within steps of the Temporaries, and if Sofie and Amanda didn't stop her, Kivi would be on her way to freedom on some other station or planet. They would never find out how much she'd embezzled to fund her new life. If she got away, she'd spend it. If she was caught, the bank would eventually absorb the balance as abandoned funds.

"Your contact? Has he found out who's smuggling her off-station?" Amanda asked.

"You think I'd keep that from you?"

Amanda looked at Sofie and then at her pad. "You're famous for not checking your messages."

Sofie checked her messages without saying anything to

defend herself. She was bad at keeping up-to-date when she was on a case. "No."

"How long will we wait for Rick?"

Sofie looked up for a media screen. There was nothing about the protests, just the regular quotas and corporate gossip. It was dangerous to keep the rest of the Mallet ignorant of the real threat of riots. When they'd interviewed people about Kivi, everyone seemed to understand there were problems in Maintenance. No one accepted that it was anything more than the normal grumbling and might not stay contained there.

"We're not waiting," Sofie said. "Stay alert for crowds and noise. We can try to slip around the problem." She checked the addresses and pointed to the one closest to the office. "Here first because we can skirt the main streets and squares. Then we get to the second one working our way through the side streets."

It would be faster going through the dark streets, but Sofie didn't like the idea of being caught there if riots broke out, and she didn't want Amanda seeing how easily she got safe passage.

"At least we aren't dressed like cops," Amanda said.

"We walk like them," Sofie said. "Don't think we'll pass as Maintenance workers."

While they were still in Support, they could pass as residents, albeit entirely too casually dressed. In Maintenance they would look like tourists.

They passed the office and moved into the first streets of Maintenance.

Amanda was scanning the streets ahead. "If we wore those orange badges, we might fit in better."

"And if we get pulled into a protest because of the badges?" Sofie asked as they passed the first square.

On the other side of the square was the real Mainte-nance. Yes, some of the stench flowed out to the streets around their office, but it was nothing compared to the reek of burned oil and desperation they'd encounter inside. Sofie was used to it from her visits to the Open Pit, but Amanda probably avoided this area like a bleak life was contagious.

"Fine," Amanda said. "Not many people around who aren't wearing them here."

They hadn't encountered any crowds as they passed through, unusual in itself, but every single person they saw had an orange patch with blue writing somewhere on their outfit.

"Not many people either way," Sofie said. "It's mid-shift, but some residents should be out on the streets."

"You think they've been warned? Something on the order of *join us or stay inside*?" Amanda increased her pace.

It was possible, and now that Amanda had said the words, Sofie noticed the feeling of bated breath. She hurried her steps. "We need to get to the address now."

As the words came out, a dull roar rose around them. The first of the protesters entered the square holding holo-placards and chanting, "Enough now!"

Amanda grabbed Sofie's arm and drew her into a service recess. "Don't move."

Their hiding place wouldn't pass muster if anyone looked directly at it, but the crowd wasn't scanning the shad-ows. They filled the square and marched in a circle. Sofie's view of the square was blocked by the bodies that passed by. Where were the riot cops? This could turn from a loud but peaceful protest into uncontrollable violence in a second. The marchers were too close for Sofie to communicate with Amanda, even though she was pressed against her body to stay as deep in the recess as possible.

The noise bounced off the walls and became an unintel-ligible wave of voices and stamping feet. Then the numbers thinned, and the sound moved off. Sofie could see the cops herding the crowd. Alongside the official authorities, a handful of gray-overalled private security from the front of the Mallet wielded stun prods — not touching anyone, just menacing the protesters who didn't follow the main crowd.

Sofie felt Amanda take a deep breath when they were suddenly alone. Her own body wasn't ready to relax even that much. She could feel the tingles in her fingers that usually meant an attack of the Fades was imminent. She had meds in her inside pocket. Could she take a dose without Amanda knowing? She had no choice but to risk it. She needed her body whole and functioning.

They stepped out of the recess. The square was empty.

"They went the opposite direction from the unit we need," Amanda said. She stepped farther into the square, leaving Sofie at the entrance.

Sofie pulled the pack of meds out as soon as Amanda turned her focus away from her. She palmed a pill and slid the pack back into her pocket.

"We should move fast," Sofie said. "I don't like the fact that the private security detail is here." She dropped the pill into her mouth and swallowed.

"There's probably an update about it," Amanda said, turning back to Sofie. "I'm not going to look, just in case we've been ordered to join the crowd control forces. Finding Kivi is critical."

Sofie tried not to show her surprise at Amanda's words. Not following procedure? Was she finally softening?

The unit they were going to search was only a street farther into Maintenance. The second one was close to the entrance to the Temporaries and meant a high chance of meeting another chanting crowd. "Lead the way."

Sofie and Amanda's pads vibrated, pinged, and rang. Nothing they could ignore.

"Get back here now," Llewelyn said. His words were quiet but there was no doubt he was not in the mood to explain.

"Karma," Amanda said. "We're paying for ignoring orders."

43

They hurried back to the office. The streets were now completely empty. Everyone must be either at work, in a protest crowd, or hiding safely at home. Sofie heard the faint rumble of the protest behind them as they left the square.

The bullpen was busier than normal. No officer or detective was off shift today. This was the mustering point, and where cops dropped their riot gear or pulled it on. No gray overalls in the room, but it didn't mean the private security company had been called off.

Llewelyn's door was open and Sofie saw him get up from behind the desk. As much as she would have liked to stop in the case room first, she knew it would just increase his anger at her and Amanda.

"Sit," he said as they walked in. "Close the door, Detective Mwendwa."

Amanda gently shut the door and flicked on the security screening.

Now sitting across from Llewelyn, Sofie's annoyance at

being called back was replaced with fear that he wouldn't let them continue. She didn't think he'd let her go back out with all the problems. But if he needed Amanda, then Sofie would be reassigned or have to go back to working alone. Kivi would get off the station. No one would take the blame for the underlying problem and the protests would erupt into riots. Cold sweat crept down her spine at the idea she would be ordered to abandon the case just as she was about to solve it.

"You're not wearing riot gear." Llewelyn made it sound like an accusation.

"We were at a critical point in the investigation," Sofie said. As much as she wanted to let Amanda talk them out of the situation, it was her case and her responsibility. "We'll pick it up now before we go out."

"A critical point?" Llewelyn asked. "You were to give me updates."

"Yes, sir. We have a suspect and she's gone to ground. We have a few locations where we believe she might be hiding prior to being smuggled off the station." She hoped he would be satisfied with a high-level summary.

"This suspect is Anna Kivi?" Llewelyn asked. The fact that he didn't need to check anything to pull the name was worrying.

"Yes. We believe she's been working with a faction involved in the manufacturing and distribution of medication. It appears they have been diverting supplies and manipulating data for profit."

"Who else is on your list?"

Amanda pulled out her pad. "I'll send you what we found," she said. "We don't have names but there is a worker in the front bays who may be involved. He is also missing.

We suspect there must be others in import and Manufacturing, but have no individuals specifically identified."

"We focused our efforts on apprehending Kivi because she would have those names," Sofie said.

"Thank you. Now I have something I can tell the Elites and Executives who call me constantly."

"If that's all," Sofie said, knowing he wouldn't have called them in for an update, "we'll head to our next location."

"No, that's not all. Your last deadline was to figure it out, now I'm saying you need to close this case in a day. If we can't tell the leaders of the protests that someone has been arrested for causing the illness, then I'm not sure we can get control back."

One day. If they found Anna Kivi at one of the two locations, it would be plenty of time to get answers to the protest leaders. Sofie wasn't convinced that an arrest would bring an end to the disruptions, but it couldn't hurt. "And our ability to move around the station? It's hard to blend in with riot gear on."

Sofie didn't look to see if Amanda agreed. The fact was, if they walked around like the cops who were trying to control the protesters, they would end up in a confrontation at some point. If they had to go into the Temporaries in riot gear, no one would talk to them.

"You will wear light protection," Llewelyn said. "I won't send you out without anything. You will be armed at all times."

Relieved that he understood, Sofie said, "Yes, sir."

"Are the Elites really calling you too often?" Amanda asked.

"Perhaps not constantly, but enough to get in the way. Why?"

"I can set a filter on your phone," she said. "Every other call from the same person will receive a busy response. Will that help?"

"I miss you, Mwendwa," Llewelyn said. "Yes, they don't give me any information or help, just complaints about delays in production or broken services."

Amanda moved to his pad and started tapping settings.

The mention of the interference reminded Sofie about Nhu and Haadiya. "I haven't heard from my liaison or Rick's. Are they calling you?"

"Eckerman and Rothwell? Not lately. I'm getting the big guns."

It was possible the Elites had given orders to their liaisons to investigate or observe the protests. They would be the perfect people to spy on activity in the Mallet. If it was true, then Sofie had seen no evidence they were interfering or even present in any way. "I guess if the Prathams and Seconds are calling you, there's no need for the Liaisons to waste their time." She wasn't going to put any ideas in Llewelyn's head by sharing her theory.

"I'm sure we'll find out soon what they've been up to," Llewelyn said. "Get back out there and find me this Kivi woman."

In the case room, Sofie dug out the light armor she'd stored there a day ago, a vest that dispersed stun shots and deflected blades. Amanda was at her locker grabbing the same equipment. While she dressed, Sofie plugged in her pad to top up the battery. Her stunners were still fully charged.

Her pad buzzed with a message as she pulled her outer clothes over the vest.

Dr. Petra Starlight. *Mabior is weakening. Judge Veltosh died.*

The pressure was going to increase on Llewelyn regardless of Amanda's filter. If an Elite died, Sofie knew the orders would change from contain and de-escalate to stun and arrest. And right now, there was no chance of stunning enough of the protesters fast enough to avoid violence.

44

One day wasn't enough to complete the investigation, but if they could find Kivi it would be plenty of time to slow or even stop the protests. If circumstances didn't keep pushing them away from following the one clue they had that might get them to Kivi, an hour would probably be enough to do that. But with a dead judge and an Elite who might be on the same track, the clinic was their next location.

"We could split up," Amanda said. "I know it's not ideal, but I could go check the units. If she's not there, we can go to the Temporaries. If she is, I'll keep her under observation until you arrive."

It was logical and Sofie wanted to say yes. She had the relationship with Dr. Starlight, so she would be faster at the clinic. But this wasn't a normal situation. If Amanda got caught up in the protests alone, it could escalate everything. And Kivi would get away.

"I think we need both of us together to be safe. That last one almost caught us off guard." She started walking toward Support. "We'll be fast at the clinic."

The encounter with the mob of protesters earlier had Sofie twitching at every sound. The relative quiet of the streets felt like a trap, and the vest seemed like too little protection.

"It's creepy, right?" Amanda said. "Like we've moved to a different station — somewhere off the Mallet where life is pleasant."

That was exactly the feeling Sofie had been trying to name. How was it possible that there was no sign of protest here when, only a few streets behind, people were hunkering down to outlast a flash of violence? What happened in Maintenance affected the Support residents — and the Elite, for that matter. "Yeah. They are in for a very rude awakening if no one is preparing."

"You think the judge's wife called Starlight?" Amanda asked.

Sofie wanted to run to the clinic, not keep up this fast stroll. But running raised alarms outside the gym. Her sense of time was distorted from all the sensory input and stress, and their deadline felt too close. "We'll ask, but maybe it wouldn't have made a difference. He was pretty far gone and hiding a condition. I'm guessing he was headed for an early death anyway."

The clinic lights came into sight. Sofie's phone pinged. Rick.

"Where are you?" he asked without waiting for a greeting.

"Near the clinic." He should have known that from her tracker.

"Someone leaked the information about the judge and Mabior. The protest leaders are accusing us of ignoring the situation until high castes are affected."

"Bullshit. They know we're investigating." She looked

around. It wasn't the most private place to have a conversation, but no one was paying attention. Amanda tipped her head, which Sofie took to mean she would keep guard and Sofie could lean on the wall.

"They just want an excuse," Rick said. "I called to let you know I'm not going to be able to answer you for a while."

"We need to go through Maintenance soon." Sofie would change their plans if going now would have a better chance of success.

"You have your gas filters with you?"

Sofie tapped her pocket and felt the hard edge of the filter. She checked with Amanda and got a *do-you-really-need-to-ask?* expression in response.

"Yes. Why?"

"We're preparing to respond. The leaders are being assholes and we need to get them around a table. So we'll flood the areas where the crowds are worst with sedative gas. Pull the leaders into a conference room and hope it breaks the momentum. If not, we're in for riots."

"When?"

Rick didn't answer right away. Sofie heard orders being delivered behind him. He'd been on riot duty for too long. If the others on his team were as tired as Rick must be... Sofie didn't want to think about the possible consequences of a mistake. The people in charge knew the risks. They were responsible.

"Okay, you have a couple of hours unless the protesters do something stupid. I'll try to give you a heads-up. You'll be fine if you get into the Temporaries by then."

He told her to be safe and ended the call.

"We need to be very quick at the clinic," Sofie said.

45

Inside the clinic, Sofie didn't wait for the receptionist to lead them to Petra. She hurried Amanda through the ward toward the doctor's workspace. There were fewer patients in the beds now, and she hoped that didn't mean more deaths. Petra was with a patient and held up a finger to acknowledge them as they passed.

Sofie had no desire to talk beside a sick person, so she nodded toward the cubicle and pulled Amanda after her. The desk was covered with thin sheets of files and charts, but Sofie didn't bother trying to read them. She didn't have basic medical knowledge, let alone the ability to decipher shorthand notes.

"Thanks for being so quick," Petra said as she walked past Sofie to sit in her chair while reading a sheet of notes. "I know it's tricky outside right now. I haven't left the clinic for three days, but I've heard about the protesters."

"It doesn't look like the news is getting through this section," Sofie said. "The situation has gone from tricky to dangerous. You might be safer here than outside in the next few days."

"I'll take your word for it, Detective."

Petra glanced at Amanda. She'd met her before, but perhaps she was getting skittish about handing out patient information now that people were dying.

"Amanda is working the case with me now," Sofie said. "She needs to hear the news too."

"Hmm," Petra said. Then, apparently deciding to trust Sofie's decision to bring Amanda along, she added, "So, of our original twelve patients who survived the first day, seven have been discharged and are well on the way to full recovery. Three are ready to be discharged, but with the current situation, we are waiting for security staff to escort them home. The conditions of the remaining two are deteriorating. I don't have a lot of confidence that they will survive the night."

"Any new people?" Sofie asked.

"Not here. Again, because of the situation outside, no one is being transported to us. There are twenty new cases in all. I have advised my colleagues on our treatment regimen and expect them to have the same success rate. It's based on too small a sample to guarantee the outcomes, but we always have hope."

Hearing that the problem hadn't gone away was troubling. If Kivi was the one messing with the meds, then why was it still happening now that she was in hiding? Sofie asked Petra for her opinion.

"Good question. If your supposition is correct, then our new supply of meds was untainted. That's why people recovered. I think she would have manually changed the supply somehow to make us think it was just a blip. Now that she's on the run, it will take some time for the useless medications to work through the system. We just don't have the people available to test every pill we have on hand."

"We'll recommend that existing supplies are checked when the case is over," Amanda said. "We can't simply wait out the supply."

"Correct," Petra said. "I have already suggested the same thing. But we currently don't have the resources to conduct testing on every batch of medications."

Another reason to put down the protests.

"Did Mrs. Veltosh contact you?" Sofie asked. They needed to get back to the important questions. "About her husband?"

"What about him?" Petra asked.

So no.

Sofie gave Petra the information. "I don't know if it would have made a difference."

Petra flipped over a record sheet. "If we knew it when he was brought in, we would have given him the meds. But he was unconscious, and the condition wasn't on his chart, so he's been unmedicated for who knows how long. Why are people so stupid?"

There was no real answer to that question. Stupid to hide a life-threatening condition? Well, she was doing it for pretty much the same reasons. Stupid to keep hiding it when it could save your life? Sofie couldn't be sure how long she'd hold out, knowing the repercussions. Thankfully, she wouldn't be in the position to worry much longer. The surgery would fix everything.

"When will we have the autopsy results?" Amanda asked.

"The wife tried to block us doing one," Petra said. "I guess I know why now. I overrode her. The health orders require a thorough examination of anyone who dies until we're over the worst of these illnesses."

"How long before you can tell us if they found anything

interesting?" Sofie wondered why Petra had dodged the question.

"Oh. Sorry, my mind wanders after too long without sleep. I'll get them on it immediately. You should hear from me in three or four hours."

"And Mabior?" Sofie asked. "Will she talk to us?"

"She won't even talk to me. I have to work with her personal physician. He doesn't care for being a go-between, but we have no choice."

"Anything we should know about her deterioration?" Amanda asked. "You called us to you for a reason."

"I want you to see this while I explain what it means." She projected a graph on the wall. "This is confidential information. If it gets out, my job is gone, and I'll probably be killed and added to the next round of cremations. In that order, if I'm lucky."

The graph showed three lines rising and falling from left to right along a timeline. Numbers went up the y-axis. It meant nothing to Sofie.

"This is generated from twenty variables of patient health. It represents the probability of mortality in the ward." Petra pointed to the lines. "Blue for all patients, red for estrogen dominant, and gray for testosterone dominant."

"Am I supposed to understand the meaning?"

Petra gestured for Sofie to wait. "This is a normal projection from six months ago. You'll notice that the lines generally trend down."

Amanda pointed to the end result. "So mostly people get better and leave? Is this one week?"

"Yes, we do it week by week because that matches an average stay. The data isn't affected by turnover. Yes, reality does follow the projections over that time. We don't know which patients will experience the ups and downs, but we can plan based on this information."

"So?" Sofie asked, anxious to leave and get to the units before the sedation gas flooded the residential areas of Maintenance.

Petra replaced the image with a new graph. This one had much higher peaks and valleys. And at the end of the time period, none of the lines hit the floor. "This is for the last few days. If this projection is correct, we will have more deaths and more patients. If we can't find a way to stop this happening, the clinics will be overwhelmed in four days."

"Catching our suspect might not fix the meds," Amanda said.

"Let's hope you're wrong," Petra said.

46

Outside the clinic, Sofie checked her pad. No message from Rick. She convinced herself it meant they had time and not that he was too busy preparing to sedate hundreds of protesters.

"What does this mean for us?" she asked Amanda. Nothing they could do would stop the onslaught of new cases Petra's analysis predicted. Those people were probably already sick and just hadn't been admitted to a clinic. Maybe catching Kivi would minimize the damage.

"Maybe nothing. We don't have the authority to pull the meds from the system," Amanda admitted.

"Maybe the supply of bad meds isn't that big," Sofie said. Despite Amanda's words, she couldn't help but feel like they should be able to do something.

"We're due some good luck," Amanda said. "I'd like to have a look at the information in the case room, where we can spread out."

"Another delay in finding Kivi," Sofie said. "Yes, I get it, we might find her faster if we do stop for a minute to see if this changes our perception of the problem. If we didn't have to worry about being caught in the crowd control tactics, I'd be happier."

"What if it's not her?" Amanda asked. She held up her hand to stall Sofie's first reaction. "I think we have the right person too, but we both know how hard it is to let go of one suspect when faced with a hint they might be innocent."

Sofie did know, but this wasn't the case here. Anna Kivi was up to her ears in this. For sure there were more conspirators, but she was their key to getting the whole scheme shut down. She tipped her head in the direction of the bullpen. "Fine. We have to pass that way, so let's see if we can find a new connection."

"One second." Amanda typed something in her pad. "Okay, I've requested a list of the people who recovered. And any records of people not reporting for a shift because of illness."

Sofie checked the time. They still had over an hour before Rick's deadline for their safe passage to the Temporaries.

IN THE CASE ROOM, Sofie sat and watched Amanda work her magic with the data. The list of people not showing up for work was huge. Too much for a quick analysis, Sofie thought. Amanda had grunted at the size of the file and then started typing.

"The protesters are calling in sick," Sofie said. "How are you going to pull them out of the list?"

"No need," Amanda said. "I'm looking for trends, and I'll remove a percentage of the results to clear the static."

Sofie kept checking the time while the data points on the wall flicked in and out. Amanda was working fast; it had only been five minutes since they walked in and turned on the privacy screen. Red dots popped up in the cloud of black. Then blue, and then everything other than the colored dots disappeared.

Amanda turned to look at Sofie. "Red is for people who knew Kivi somehow, worked with her, had a social connection — very few in that category — or had business dealings with her. Blue is for multiple connections."

"And these are people who have recovered, or called in sick?" Sofie was captured with the pattern. The information had been there all along, but she hadn't thought to look for this kind of link.

"And people who are still in the clinic, and the people who died. See, she met with Mabior at an art exhibit, and Judge Veltosh belongs to her photography club."

So, a pattern, but no clear pointer for our next move. What other connections could there be?

"Maybe I'm not seeing something you are," Sofie said. "We need to get back to the search soon, but am I missing something?"

Amanda shook her head and stepped closer to the wall as if she would notice something she couldn't from two feet away. "I think we need to ask a different question. This is the right data, I'm sure of that."

What questions hadn't they asked? "Any way to find out if the people calling in sick with a connection to Kivi have underlying conditions?"

"Not without their medical records. We don't have time for that."

Bindes might help get the records, but he was likely hunkered down with the rest of the Maintenance people. "What about partnerships? You pulled out people she had a business connection with. Were any of them partners?"

"Good question. Give me a second." Amanda added

back the full set of data points. Then five green dots appeared along with the red and blue ones. Three over-lapped with the originals.

"Let's look at the people who have more than one connection," Sofie said. Her gut told her they were on a good track, just not what it was.

"One of them has a partnership with her to provide business advice. I'm guessing Kivi brought in the money and contact, but the partner did the advising. Name's Maria Ali — called in sick the last two days."

"She could be on the run with Kivi," Sofie said. "The other two?"

"She worked with Deva Lu. He owned a stim-juice bar with her — they sold it a few months ago."

"And he's dead," Sofie said. "I didn't get any indication he was involved when we interviewed him."

"The final one is a Support analyst. They registered a partnership agreement, but nothing came of the business," Amanda said.

Sofie checked the time again. This was eating into their remaining time to solve the case and pushing them danger-ously close to the crowd being sedated. Her gut was still saying this was important, but it kept slipping through her grasp. And Kivi could be getting on a shuttle right now.

"I guess we should head out," Amanda said. "This can wait for the court case."

Sofie closed her eyes to try to force one more idea from her subconscious. It didn't work. "Fine, save this and then clear the data. I don't want anyone realizing what we've looked at."

Amanda turned the projector off and shut down her pad.

"Wait," Sofie said, turning back to the wall. "It's the business relationships." Her subconscious finally popped a question into her head. "Not the ones we found. She made sure they were all closed up before she planned her escape. Who owned the units she used for business before they became empty?"

The wall lit up with two names as Amanda completed the query.

"Do they own any others?" Sofie asked.

Four units in Maintenance popped up, all retail and listed as empty. Kivi was too smart to stick to unassigned units. Too many chances that neighbors would notice and report something fishy. But units ready to lease out? Nothing odd about people going in and out of them. "We've got her. She's going to be in one of those, I'll bet my career."

47

When Sofie checked the newsfeeds, she breathed a little easier. The protests were stalled because every one of the protesters was sleeping off the effects of the gas. The crowd control team was sorting through the participants to pull out the leaders.

No longer needing to hurry to avoid crowds, Sofie called Rick as they headed out of the office. "We think Anna Kivi is hiding in Maintenance. Any chance you've seen her?"

"I'm busy coordinating the transport," he said. "Send me her image and I'll scan the crowds for her."

If Anna Kivi was lying unconscious on a street somewhere, their luck had turned. "On its way."

"I'll let you know. Where are you?"

Sofie turned to Amanda. "Can we use facial recognition on the vids of the protesters? Maybe she's been hiding in the crowd."

Amanda nodded and headed back to the case room.

"We're going in to search for her," she said to Rick when she was alone. "It's safe now, right?"

"Yeah, we didn't get all of them, but enough to make things quiet down here for a couple of hours."

"What's happening to the people who were only following the leaders?"

"They're being left in place. The higher-ups think it will send a message."

Or set them off again as soon as they wake up. "What do you think?"

"Not my job to correct my superiors," he said.

The unnamed superior must be standing close enough to hear Rick. "I get it. We'll let you know what's going on as soon as we have news."

Taking the protest out of the equation didn't give Sofie any more time. Llewelyn wanted someone in custody in less than twenty hours, and they hadn't made any real headway since his demand.

"I've set the query, and the system will alert me if it gets a hit." Amanda glanced back toward the Support section. "We're assuming she's in hiding, but what if she's just moving around in disguise?"

It could be true, but a system-wide facial recognition scan would take too long. "If we had time and resources, I'd have the chance to follow more than one theory. Look, let's go check the units; shouldn't take us long since we don't have to dodge protests. If we find nothing, we start looking for her across the station." If times were normal, Sofie would have a Mallet-wide alert on Kivi. The alert would only go to the cops, but they'd have her in custody within hours. Right now, there were so few cops on regular duty that Kivi could walk past them without a disguise and wearing a name tag without getting grabbed.

. . .

THE FIRST UNIT had an *opening soon* sign on the door. When they looked inside, there was nothing. The new tenant had painted the interior an acid yellow that was still drying. The second unit contained three Accept protectors. Sofie told them to find authorized units after interviewing them. No women had come by in the last two days. They were gathering to prepare to help in the aftermath of the protests.

The third unit showed signs of recent occupation. A bedroll, some empty water containers, and food wrappers. Whoever had been here was gone.

"We need someone to verify if it was Kivi," Sofie said.

Amanda held up a strand of blond hair. "No. Probably just this." She ran the DNA and confirmed that Kivi had been in the unit. "So we're close."

"Is she coming back, though?" Sofie asked. "There are no supplies waiting for her. If she's abandoned this hiding place, where did she go?" Hopefully not straight onto a shuttle.

"We can pull the security recordings," Amanda said.

"She's smart enough to have altered them, but it's worth a try." Sofie picked through the piles of trash, hoping for some clue about Kivi's whereabouts, while Amanda requested the security footage.

Her phone buzzed and she answered it without looking at the ID. "Yes?"

"Detective Allen?" It was Petra Starlight.

"Yes. Do you have something for us?" Sofie looked up for Amanda, but she was staring at her pad.

"I lost another patient. Suddenly. He was improving and I'd hoped to discharge him today."

Another death was tragic but didn't get them closer to Kivi. "I'm sorry, Petra, you clearly care about your patients." The words sounded patronizing in her ears, but she'd meant it sincerely. Some doctors treated diseases, some treated patients. Petra was one of the best at doing both. "Does it change the statistics at all?"

"No. But it does confirm the trend. I've had notice of ten more patients in Maintenance alone."

Just what we need, more pressure to get this case solved. "We're close to catching our woman."

"That's what I called about, actually. The patient had a visitor. I'm worried that she had something to do with his death."

Sofie held her breath and tapped Amanda's elbow to get her attention. She set the call on speaker so she wouldn't have to relay the information later. Then she let go of the breath and asked, "What did this visitor look like?"

"Do you have a picture of your suspect?" Petra asked.

Amanda nodded and tapped her screen.

"You should have it from Detective Mwendwa."

"Just a second. Yes, it's here."

"Is that the woman who visited?" Sofie wished she didn't have to ask.

"Yes. I think she must have done something to kill him."

"How long since she left?" Kivi wasn't hiding. Why did she need that patient dead? If she was hoping to distract them into going back to the clinic, it wasn't enough. In fact, it pushed them harder after Kivi, not away from her.

"I didn't note the time because we were dealing with the patient. But I'd say no more than a half hour ago."

Not enough time to reach the Temporaries unless she'd given up on hiding her face and just ran for it. "Can you get tests done fast?"

"I'll draw blood and do my own tests. There are no marks on the body and no specific markers for any poison. That narrows it down."

"Can you send the patient details to us?" Sofie stepped outside the unit as she talked, needing space around her.

"Yes. I'll let you know what the tests reveal. Please find this person before we lose more patients."

Sofie promised, something she rarely did. But they almost had Kivi. If she'd been in Support that recently, she must be on the move now and coming toward them.

Her pad pinged, and she found the patient's name and recent medical records. Not any of the names they found connected to Kivi, but there must be a link. Otherwise, why would Kivi risk discovery by moving around the Mallet?

48

"Now we can find her," Amanda said. "I'll grab her image from the security footage outside the clinic and track her through the cameras."

Something good has come from the man's death.

Sofie checked the newsfeeds, hoping Kivi might be in the background of a shot, but no luck. Apparently, a square filled with sleeping bodies didn't rate coverage. It would still take a while to track Kivi through the cameras. Amanda was good, but she'd be slowed by getting permission for some of the footage.

"I don't think we should just stand here," she said. "It was only a half hour ago. We should head toward her."

Amanda pointed at the pad. "She didn't come this way. I found her heading for the front Temporaries. She dumped her jacket in a recess and wrapped her hair in a scarf. It didn't fool me."

Why had she gone into the clinic without a disguise? "Do you have her on camera now?"

"She's in the first bay. You think she's going to leave from there?"

Sofie had dismissed the possibility of Kivi going out the front early in the case. It still didn't make sense. There weren't a lot of shuttles she could be smuggled on. The ore transport ships went back empty, which meant no atmosphere outside the control section. Any shuttle with people wouldn't work because they were usually transporting teams who knew each other, or Elite family members on business.

"No, but she might be trying to finish something she started with that technician. He's gone, but someone must have replaced him."

"We'll never make it before she leaves," Amanda said. "We could get close, though."

"Keep your eye on her movements and we'll go toward Support. She has to come through there."

Now they hurried. If they could grab Kivi before she got near her escape route, then maybe they could stop the madness.

"*Fuck*, I almost missed her." Amanda was jogging alongside Sofie, and at the same time keeping her eyes on the screen. "She's wearing blue overalls. We'll lose her if she finds a crowd."

Good thing the protesters were all unconscious. Sofie asked Amanda the question she'd been considering while they moved. "Why did she go into the clinic without a disguise?"

"I've been wondering that too."

"She got to the clinic without the cameras noticing," Sofie said. "Whatever disguise she used must have been easy to ditch."

"Or she's arrogant enough to think she knows where the surveillance is focused? Or she thinks we're all involved in the protest suppression?" Amanda checked her pad again and nudged Sofie into a side street. "Is she some kind of sociopath? Doesn't think the rules apply to her, or that she'll get punished?"

Like an Elite would think?

It took a lot of ego to do what Kivi had done. But she'd decided to run when the investigation got close, so she understood she could be caught. "I didn't peg her that way."

"So she didn't screw up." Amanda came to a stop. "*Fuck.* She's behind us."

"How?"

Amanda slid her finger across the screen. "She got into one of the protest squares. They're waking up. Sorry."

"Not your fault. Not everyone can run and watch a screen at the same time. We'll double back." The last thing Sofie expected was to feel sympathy for Amanda. The woman never made a mistake. She hadn't this time, either.

"She might be going into the dark streets." Amanda tapped on her screen. "We should head toward the last unit on our list. I think she's headed there."

"Still in the overalls?"

Amanda nodded and started moving back in the direction they'd just come from. "I think I know why she did it."

"What?" Kivi had done so many things Sofie couldn't pick one.

"Went to the clinic without a disguise. She wanted the guy to know it was her."

Sofie followed Amanda. If she was right, then maybe they could use Kivi's ego against her. "That does jibe with what Deva Lu said. He thought she was nasty for the fun of it." At least that was the way Sofie interpreted his comment.

"That means if we corner her, she'll be dangerous," Amanda said.

"Be ready to stun her at any provocation," Sofie said. "I'll deal with the paperwork if we injure or kill her, but we need her alive. She's just part of the problem. We need names. And she'll know how much of the useless meds are in the system. Maybe save some lives to get some points for the trial."

Amanda checked her screen. "She's disappeared again. Give me a second."

Sofie kept watch while Amanda worked. If the protesters were stirring, the streets would be dangerous for two lone cops.

"Got her," Amanda announced. "She changed again. This time into street clothes. Ready to head to the Temporaries."

"We need to get her before she enters," Sofie said. "Until I know who her contact is, we have very little chance of finding her before she's out of our reach."

49

S ofie's pad pinged. She fought the urge to ignore whoever it was. They were so close and if they gave Kivi the chance, she'd disappear.

"Answer it so we can go," Amanda snapped.

It was Petra. Sofie nodded to Amanda to start leading the way. "Doctor."

"I have a result for you."

"Can it wait? We're close to an arrest."

"Most of the details are of no use to you," Petra said. "I'll need time to write it up in a way the courts can use the information, anyway. But there's one thing you need to hear. For your safety."

Sofie followed Amanda around a corner. She was holding her pad out and glancing down to the screen and then up to scan the street. If Kivi saw them, she'd have the advantage because neither of them was paying full attention.

"Yes?"

"The full test results will take a little while, but I

followed a hunch and tested for five of the most likely poisons immediately. It turns out my hunch was right."

Sofie wished she could hurry Petra along, but even in this situation the doctor's status required a measure of respect. And to be fair, she was used to taking her time with a diagnosis. "You know how she killed him?"

"Yes. We don't have any natural poisons on the Mallet. Not including the atmosphere in some sections, of course."

Sofie turned another corner and realized they were skirting the edges of the dark streets.

"But we do import chemicals that can be turned into a poison. And of course, almost anything is poisonous at the right — or should I say wrong — dosage."

I don't need a lecture. Sofie kept the thought inside. "Doctor, I hate to rush you, but we may be about to find her."

"Yes, of course. The one she used is called pneumotx. It simply stops the lungs from working. It is effective within three seconds."

If Kivi had this on her, she couldn't be caught by just stunning her. They would have to make sure she couldn't deploy it. "What do you advise?"

"It's a spray, and it must be inhaled. Skin contact doesn't work."

"Will a normal gas filter deal with it?"

"Yes. But you must be wearing it. Are you equipped?"

Thanks to Rick's warning, they both had filters in their gear. "Yes. We will try to disable her. If we hit the container with a stunner, will it be a problem?"

"I'd avoid that," Petra said. "If it breaks, the contents could kill any person within a ten-block radius. And I'm sure you can guess how that will sit with these protesters."

"Thank you, Doctor." Sofie ended the call and told Amanda to stop.

She gave Amanda the news, and they inserted the gas filters into their nostrils and pulled the mouth guard down. They both looked at Amanda's pad to check Kivi's location.

"She's not going into hiding," Amanda said. "Her path isn't leading to any of the units we identified."

"You think she risked bringing the poison along with her?"

"It's just as dangerous to her," Amanda said. "And they would scan her for something like weapons, right? Even a smuggler wouldn't want to take a chance that the shuttle would explode."

"I don't know. It wasn't smart to go back and kill the guy."

Usually by this point in an investigation, Sofie had a clear understanding of the suspect, or at the very least, enough knowledge to predict their moves. Usually she had Rick and more than a couple of days to finish the job.

"We have to assume she has it," Amanda said. "Anything else we need to prepare?"

"No. We're safe as long as we don't breathe it in." Sofie nodded to the pad. "Let's go directly to the Temporaries. I can call my contact to see if he's got an update on who she's meeting."

"You think it's worth the risk of losing her?" Amanda was still staring at her pad.

"I think the risk is bigger if we don't find her there," Sofie said. "If she gets to her exit point before we find her, we'll lose any hope of catching her. That's what this case has been from the start: hoping to find something before it's too late."

Amanda stuffed her pad into a jacket pocket and started walking. "Okay, let's go. We should beat her there. I think she's been trying to see if she's being followed. It's slowed her down."

Sofie picked up her pace. Running now was worth the risk of bringing attention.

50

Torque hadn't had the name of the smuggler for her. Sofie wondered if they would ever find out who Kivi paid to get her off the Mallet. And if it mattered as long as they stopped her from leaving.

The streets had a subdued feeling about them. Shift change started before Amanda and Sofie approached the entrance to the Temporaries, slowing them down. But no one looked up from the ground as they hurried past. No one grumbled. Far from being reassuring, it felt like the count-down to an explosion. And no one else could see it coming.

"What's the plan when we get inside?" Amanda asked when they came to a stop within sight of the Temporaries. "I haven't caught her on the facial recognition for a while."

"We still need to be cautious in there. I'm not sure anyone is willing to trade a killer for a slew of stupid contract-violation lawsuits from clients. Even if the price includes a few lives."

"Okay, but that doesn't answer my question." Amanda flicked her finger across the screen of her pad. "Damn it. I think she went through the dark streets and changed clothes. The drones and cameras there are mostly showing static."

Sofie moved closer to look at the screen. "Clothing didn't fool you before. You think she had time for some mods?"

"Not full-on ones. But there are some temporary patches circulating that fool the scans. If she used something like that until she got into the Temps, we'll see it on her face."

The outgoing Temporaries was under the same surveillance as the rest of the Mallet. The difference was that their feed was blocked from the cops without a warrant. And Sofie didn't have time to get one.

"We go to the bays," Sofie said. "It's not the one my contact controls, so that only leaves four to check. No matter how fast she moved, we can't be that far behind her."

Amanda pulled up the floor plans of the section. "We should stick together, yes?"

Sofie nodded. If Kivi had that spray with her, it would take both of them to subdue her safely. "We work our way from the closest to the farthest bay. Not a complete search without the paperwork. But I'm hoping we notice something fishy somewhere. Or if the universe is feeling generous, we'll see her."

"Are we using emergency powers?" Amanda asked.

Technically, the danger Kivi represented didn't rise to a level that would allow them to use emergency powers. But she was a danger to the residents of the Temporaries and if handled wrong, this could easily escalate to a hostage situation. Or, if Kivi used her poison, to multiple deaths. Of people who had value, this time. "We can't worry about that. It's for the lawyers to work out after we catch her."

"And if she goes free?" Amanda asked. "Look, I know

you think I'm too ambitious for my own good, but we need the charges to stick. If she gets out on a technicality, the protests will kick off again no matter what agreement their leaders sign."

Sofie knew all this. "We need to be invited in," she said. "If we were in pursuit, not just following a hunch that she's in there but actually chasing her, we'd be fine."

"You think your contact will invite you in?" Amanda asked. "We can't wait long."

Why did she have to revert to her annoying mode when Sofie needed to think? "We can try." She sent a message to Torque to call her. "Keep watching the entrance, maybe we'll avoid all this by grabbing her outside the section, or following her in."

Torque responded to her text immediately. "What can I do for you, Detective?"

"I don't have time for small talk. I'm recording this conversation. I need to come in after a suspect and I don't have a warrant."

"This is the woman who you suspect is behind the sickness and deaths?"

"Yes. She might have deadly intentions for someone inside your section." She wished she could just ask him for permission, but if there were repercussions for Torque from his employer, he needed an out that didn't include withdrawing the invitation and destroying her case.

"What exactly do you intend to do while searching?" Torque knew the game well enough to be cagey about his approval.

"We believe she is headed to an accomplice in bay two, three, four, or five."

"You have my invitation," Torque said. "Please proceed

with caution and respect for the contract that governs the Temporaries."

Sofie ended the call. Torque sent her a message. *If you don't find her here, erase the recording.*

51

They spotted Kivi in bay four. Sofie noticed her as she darted from one storage space to another. She was wearing a coverall to match the legitimate workers, and a cap covering her hair, but the way she moved gave her away.

"Have you ever walked though one of these places?" Sofie asked Amanda. She knew how to match the pace and cross the streams of workers and equipment from her last visit.

"No." Amanda didn't turn away from watching the entrance to the space Kivi had entered. "There's a trick, right? Will we be able to keep an eye out in case she leaves?"

"Not both of us," Sofie said. "You hang on to my hand. I'll get us there, you keep watch."

Beside her, Amanda stiffened. She wouldn't like being dependent. Sofie didn't care. This was the only way it would work.

Sofie slowed just before the entrance to the loading area Anna Kivi had entered. The foot traffic here was light, only a few people walking a path to and from the waiting shuttle.

"From here, just don't bump into anyone," she said, letting go of Amanda.

It was odd that no one had approached to ask what the hell they were doing interfering with the workers, but she wouldn't delve into why. Being free to do their jobs would make capturing Kivi before she killed anyone else or fled much easier.

Sofie leaned in to scan the area. The space was about a hundred meters square, filled with stacks of crates in rows. Plenty of hiding spots. No sign of Kivi. "We should be able to keep her isolated from the workers," she said.

They slipped past the entrance and then separated, Amanda taking the left-hand rows, Sofie taking the right. Sofie watched as Amanda moved toward the back, turning quickly to peek into each side path between rows and then move on. Sofie did the same.

Every time she turned to look into a row, she held her breath. Knowing that the filter should protect her from the poison they suspected Kivi carried didn't keep her from imagining all kinds of other weapons. If *she* had to flee the Mallet this way? She'd have stunners and a blade along with the spray.

There were twenty rows on each side of the space, with the last crates up against the back wall. Sofie kept moving, spinning into each row to find it empty. The few steps between, she kept scanning behind in case Kivi found a way to slip past.

"Got her," Amanda called.

Sofie sprinted to join Amanda, holding her weapon ready to fire at the slightest provocation. Kivi was backed against the wall, a spray bottle in one hand, the other held out to stop them advancing.

"I'll use this if you come closer." Kivi's gaze skipped from one face to the other. "I won't let you take me in."

It wasn't her choice. Sofie lowered her stunner and stepped ahead of Amanda, careful not to get in the way if it came to using weapons. She stayed far enough back to avoid being sprayed — she hoped.

"It's over," she said. "Coming in and telling us what you know is your only choice."

Kivi laughed, the sound edging on maniacal. "You have no idea what choices I have."

Sofie trusted Amanda to stay out of the conversation and not fire unless it was necessary. She focused all of her attention on the woman in front of her. Something had pushed Kivi close to the edge.

"Where were you going?" she asked, hoping to bring Kivi closer to a rational state. "That's what you planned, right? Getting smuggled off the station? You must have a lot of credit stashed."

"You can't trick me into telling you what I know," Kivi said. "Yes, I was leaving. Yes, it would be unauthorized. But I would be free, and they wouldn't be able to find me easily."

They?

"Why did you do it?" Sofie asked.

"Credits. Enough to get off this shithole before... no, I won't tell you."

This was not the answer to her question. More credits, freedom, they were the most common motives on the Mallet. Messing with the medications was not the usual kind of crime.

What had she meant by before? There was no indication that anything dire was coming to the Mallet. There was enough trouble already on the station. Sure, there was unrest, but taking Kivi in should derail the protests, and things would go back to normal.

"Why the meds?"

"It's what I had to work with. They said I could do what I wanted to stir things up." She clamped her lips tight.

"If you tell us what's going on, we can protect you," Sofie said. She took a step closer. Kivi didn't react.

"No, you can't."

She wasn't getting off-station now, so anything she'd set up would affect her as much as the people she'd planned to leave behind. Sofie didn't think stating that was the best way to calm her down.

"Okay. But shouldn't they pay for what's happened? I mean to you, Anna."

"I can't make them pay. No one can." Her body slumped. "I can't be here when it happens."

"When what happens?" Sofie asked. "If you tell us, we can stop it."

"No one can stop it." Kivi looked at the floor. She started talking again, but quietly, like she'd forgotten about Sofie and Amanda. "I could have left, but I had to go kill one more asshole. I should have left him to them. It was stupid, but I wanted him dead for what he did."

Sofie moved while Kivi argued with herself. Four steps and she had Kivi's outstretched arm in her grip. She pulled to twist the woman to face the wall.

Kivi put her foot against the wall and pressed back.

Sofie tried to grab Kivi's other hand, the one holding the aerosol container. She had to get her under control. They were too tangled up for Amanda to use the stunner.

Kivi pushed harder against the wall and then lifted the aerosol and sprayed her own face.

Sofie let go and stepped back.

"Now they can't hurt me."

Kivi gasped and then went still.

52

Two hours later, Sofie sat beside Amanda in Llewelyn's office, giving their report.

"Any idea what she meant about 'something is coming' or who 'they' are?" Llewelyn asked.

Sofie's initial thoughts while they waited for the medical team to arrive were that Kivi was unbalanced. But now, she wasn't so sure. "We know she was working for someone," she said, "but not if her employers were the mysterious 'they'. And the threat? The only thing I can come up with is she thought there would be riots. Maybe she didn't realize we'd use her arrest to calm things down."

Llewelyn turned to Amanda. "Mwendwa, you think the same?"

Sofie waited for Amanda to undermine her. This was the perfect opportunity to steal the credit and get her promotion. Just because Sofie didn't want to advance didn't mean she was happy to have someone else take credit for her successes.

Amanda looked up to the ceiling and gave a slow blink. Then she turned her gaze to Llewelyn. "We don't have enough information to make a decent prediction. Maybe with her death it all goes away. We'll know if it stops the illness from increasing soon. Maybe she meant a station-wide epidemic? If whatever had her that scared is coming from off the Mallet, we don't have the power to investigate."

"Maybe one of the Prathams would know," Sofie said. "Their partners must be keeping an eye on the Mallet, making sure nothing disrupts commerce."

"I think we'll leave that to the Elites themselves," Llewelyn said. "Or perhaps your contacts might be amenable to doing a little research for the benefit of the Mallet?"

"I'll give it some thought. It won't happen if we just ask. Maybe Rick?"

"It's not urgent," Llewelyn said. "We're all busy making sure the media use the result to calm things down instead of inflaming tempers."

"We need to stay alert," Sofie said. "There are too many maybes, and that means trouble on its own."

Llewelyn checked his screen and nodded at whatever he read. "If we've brought an end to the medical crisis, we should know by tomorrow. Your Dr. Starlight predicted four days before the system is overwhelmed, right?"

"I'll ask her to keep us updated," Sofie said. "Kivi's job included analyzing trends. She could have created the conditions that made it look like things were getting worse when they weren't."

"She wasn't planning to be here to face the consequences," Llewelyn said. "She may have set something to run automatically."

Still, nothing they could do but wait. Sofie hated not closing the case completely. "One thing is different," she said. "The front Temporaries. Is that private security team a long-term thing?"

"You think the Elites already know what's coming and are setting up defenses?" He made it sound like paranoia. "They were helpful with protest control."

Not an answer to her question. Sofie knew better than to push for more. "Okay, then what's happening with the protests?"

"You want your partner back?" Llewelyn asked. "It's going to take a few days to be sure, but the news of Kivi's arrest and the takedown of the protest leaders seems to have cooled tempers."

"You arrested them?" Amanda asked. "I thought the plan was to get them into negotiations."

Llewelyn checked his screen again. They were about to be dismissed. "We tried negotiating," he said. "It turned out they didn't like being sedated. A few blows were exchanged, and arrests happened. We'll let them go tomorrow if nothing else kicks off and they are ready to take a softer stance."

"And Rick?" Sofie asked.

"He'll be dismissed from Shehata's team today."

Amanda stood and smoothed her jacket. "I think Sofie and I have earned a few days off, then."

How did she know that was my next question? How had she changed it from a request to a reward?

"Fair enough," Llewelyn said. "Write up your reports and take three days. There's one more thing."

He waited until Amanda took her seat again.

"We can't ignore Kivi's threats. When you return to duty, you'll form a task force. You two and Rick. Between you there's a lot of skill and instinct. You'll need it. We can't ignore this threat. We have to know exactly what it is, or be completely sure it's just ranting from a disturbed mind."

He dismissed them and turned to his screen.

BACK IN THE CASE ROOM, Sofie started clearing the few hard copies into a pile and opened her notes for reference. Amanda logged into the system and started typing up her report from memory.

"Thanks for the days off," Sofie said. "I'm going to sleep for all three days."

"I might squeeze in a couple of gym visits," Amanda said. "But yeah. I feel like I haven't stopped for days."

"That's because we haven't," Sofie said. "And we won't get much rest when we get back."

"I'll worry about that later," Amanda said. "Although, I get the feeling we'll need to polish up our diplomacy skills. If there is some big plot to uncover, it won't be coming from the lower castes."

Sofie sent a message to Dr. Bindes to let him know she had time for the procedure now and asked him if he could make it happen. Writing up her report and reviewing Amanda's wouldn't take long. There were only a couple of follow-up tasks to schedule before she went off-line to recover. She sent a message to Dr. Starlight to let her know Llewelyn was her contact about the trends or any other news.

Rick could give the boss of the dark streets a heads-up about the possible trouble on the way. Sofie felt like she owed it to him for the protection he'd extended her lately. And he might end up solving their problem for them. After all, what's bad for the Mallet was bad for the dark streets.

53

Sofie left the office as soon as she hit submit on her case report. She met Dr. Bindes in a small unit not far from her quarters. The place was set up for her operation and would be sterilized and closed down as soon as she left. No way to trace anyone involved, including herself.

She was greeted by a woman covered from head to toe in surgical protective gear. All Sofie saw were her eyes, a normal, indistinguishable brown. "Three days is the minimum. I recommend another two days to be sure you recuperate completely."

She couldn't ask for more time off. The task force was important, and she didn't want to make up a lie for Llewelyn anyway. Would the doctor stop the procedure if Sofie couldn't take more time? "Okay, I'll make sure I call in sick for two days past my leave." She had no problem lying to this stranger. The first couple of days back would be setting up the task force, so more like rest than work.

Bindes joined them from where he'd been examining the set up. "You prepared your place for recovery?"

Sofie nodded. She'd brought in three days' worth of meal packages and cleaned every surface, and the sheets on her bed. "I'm ready. How long will this take?"

"We'll go in through your nasal cavity," the anonymous doctor responded. "The incisions will not be visible. You have the spray to promote healing."

The source of the Fades was in her brain. Not anywhere particularly difficult to reach, but they would be implanting a device that would stimulate the production of a hormone somewhere else in her body.

The technical terms didn't matter to Sofie. The device would last well beyond her lifespan. There were no side effects, and after she healed from the surgery, she would never have to take a med for her condition again. The recovery time was to ensure the thing didn't shift while her body grew new tissue around it.

Bindes would transport her to her home while she was unconscious and settle her in. Three days of minimal move-ment and she should be fine. Pretty much what she'd told Amanda she'd do, sleep for the three she had off.

"Headaches are normal," the doctor said. "If they last more than a day, contact Dr. Bindes. Dizziness may occur when you start to move around. It's positional vertigo and will pass."

Bindes led Sofie to the table and helped her stretch out. "Anything you'd like to say before you go under?"

What could she say? Would she miss him? He'd been part of her life for so long, it would be odd if she didn't. She could always drop by the Open Pit if she needed some off-the-books medical advice, research, or just plain gossip. What did he want to hear? "Thanks for arranging this. I'll see you when it's done."

Someone started counting. Sofie breathed in a cool mist, then everything faded away into a deep, blissful quiet.

WANT MORE?

Who is the mysterious entity behind the riots on The Mallet? Use the QR code to go to Red Lined and join Sofie in the final battle for their home.

If you enjoyed reading White Noise, please consider helping other readers to find the story by leaving a review.

~

FREE EBOOK

Claim your copy of Running the Game when you use the
QR code below to sign up for my newsletter and cheer on
Pen as she vies for a commission in the military.

ALSO BY PA WILSON

For more books by P A Wilson

Use the QR code below or go to pawilson.ca

ABOUT THE AUTHOR

Perry Wilson is a Canadian author based in Vancouver, BC who has big ideas and an itch to tell stories. Having spent some time on university, a career, and life in general, she returned to writing in 2008 and hasn't looked back since (well, maybe a little, but only while parallel parking).

She is a member of the Vancouver Writers Social Group, The Royal City Literary Arts Society, and The Surrey Writing Workshop. Perry has self-published several novels. She writes the Madeline Journeys, a fantasy series about a high-powered lawyer who finds herself trapped in a magical world, the Quinn Larson Quests, which follows the adventures of a wizard named Quinn who must contend with volatile fae in the heart of Vancouver, and the Charity Deacon Investigations, a mystery thriller series about a private eye who tends to fall into serious trouble with her cases, and The Riverton Romances, a series based in a small town in Oregon, one of her favorite states. Her stand-alone novels are Breaking the Bonds, Closing the Circle, and The Dragon at The Edge of The Map.

For more information
www.pawilson.ca
pawilson@pawilson.ca

ACKNOWLEDGMENTS

People think that the process of writing is solitary. That's not the case for me. I have help from so many people it would be hard to acknowledge everyone, but I'll give it a try.

The support and inspiration I get from my writer's groups is incalculable. The Vancouver Writers Social Group opens my mind to other ways of telling a story. The Royal City Literary Arts Society gives me the opportunity to meet and share with other writers who have more knowledge than I do. The Other 11 Months group is where I learn about getting the words on the page. And my critique group who helps me find the best parts of the story I want to tell. Thanks to all of the members of these great groups.

Last of all, but definitely a huge part of the process, my beta readers. These are the people who love stories and are willing, and more than able, to tell me if my finished story is ready for you, my readers.